The Hot List

Also by Hillary Homzie:

Things Are Gonna Get Ugly

The Hot List

Hillary Homzie

NEW YORK   LONDON   TORONTO   SYDNEY

This book is a work of fiction. Any references to historical events, real people, or real locales are used fictitiously. Other names, characters, places, and incidents are the product of the author's imagination, and any resemblance to actual events or locales or persons, living or dead, is entirely coincidental.

ALADDIN M!X

Simon & Schuster Children's Publishing Division

1230 Avenue of the Americas, New York, NY 10020

First Aladdin M!X edition March 2011

Copyright © 2011 by Hillary Homzie

All rights reserved, including the right of reproduction in whole or in part in any form.

ALADDIN is a trademark of Simon & Schuster, Inc., and related logo is a registered trademark of Simon & Schuster, Inc.

ALADDIN M!X and related logo are registered trademarks of Simon & Schuster, Inc

For information about special discounts for bulk purchases, please contact Simon & Schuster Special Sales at 1-866-506-1949 or business@simonandschuster.com.

The Simon & Schuster Speakers Bureau can bring authors to your live event.

For more information or to book an event contact the Simon & Schuster Speakers Bureau at 1-866-248-3049 or visit our website at www.simonspeakers.com.

Designed by Lisa Vega

The text of this book was set in Adobe Caslon.

Manufactured in the United States of America 0211 OFF

10 9 8 7 6 5 4 3 2 1

Library of Congress Control Number 2010934261

ISBN 978-1-4424-0657-5 (pbk)

ISBN 978-1-4424-3034-1 (eBook)

To the dessert divas known as my writing group

Acknowledgments

First off, a huge thanks to my editors, Alyson Heller and Liesa Abrams, who really know how to brainstorm, how to inspire thoughtful revision, and to have fun. I feel bow-down lucky to have you on my side.

A huge shout-out goes to my agent, Sean McCarthy, for his attention to this book right from the start.

Thanks to Lisa Gottfried for our weekly babysitting swaps, which allowed me the space to complete this book.

I'm also so lucky to have fantastic early readers. Leslie Farwell, Jenny Pessereau, and Sherry Smith pumped me way up while lovingly delivering the truth. Steven Arvanites read *The Hot List* more than once and indulged me in many late night talks. The red licorice definitely helped! Alexandria LaFaye helped refine the beginning, while Rachel Rodriguez was an astute online critique partner, and Erin Dealey set me straight on the real deal in middle school.

Jonah, Ari, and Micah, thanks for your daily insights

into the secret life of boys. My husband, Matt, is another great reader, and the fourth of four boys (so he kind of knows boys), as well as meal-maker when deadlines approach. I love you all!

Chapter One

Maddie and I came up with the Hot List one morning after a sleepover at my house. Lounging on my bed, we flipped through magazines, sucking down wild cherry Slurpees and pigging out on M&M's. All but the red ones. If you eat those, you have to tell the truth.

"If we're going to write up a hot list," I said. "We should use something special."

"Definitely," said Maddie.

I bounced over to the door and closed it so it clicked all the way shut. Then I opened my desk drawer and pulled a pen out of my keepsake bin. "Here," I said, holding up the pen. Two summers ago, Maddie got it for my tenth birthday. It was purple with little sparkles of gold.

"Perfect!" said Maddie. She tucked her chin-length hair behind her ears.

"Okay, I need those red ones now," I said, pointing to the pile of M&M's.

Maddie divided them up. Eight for her and eight for me, and then she began counting. "One. Two. Three." We both popped a couple into our mouths at the exact same moment. "It's truth time!" she shouted—although her mouth was so full of little round candies, it sounded more like this: "mmmitsthtime!"

"I'll go first," I said, bravely uncapping the glitter pen and sitting down on the shag rug carpet. "Then you. But no peeking until we're done."

Hopping down off the bed, Maddie plopped down next to me.

"Move away," I commanded.

Maddie didn't budge.

"Hello! Back on the bed, or go to the other side of the carpet."

Maddie scooted back a little.

"More."

Finally, Maddie moved to the opposite edge of the carpet. "Sophie, you're paranoid. Don't you trust me?" She jumped up for a moment, pretended to peer at my paper, and then sat back down.

"Of course," I said, smiling, as I quickly wrote down our top five names:

SOPHIE'S PERSONAL HOT LIST

1) Hayden Carus
2) Matt James
3) Bear Arvanites
4) Tyson Blandes
5) Kirk Davies

"There—done," I said, folding up the paper. "Your turn." I tossed the pen to Maddie, and she actually caught it. "Good catch."

Maddie retucked her hair behind her ears and wrote down her hot list. Only she wrote in swirly, fancy letters. I was really proud of Maddie being so arty, but I got embarrassed for her when she did calligraphy at school. I didn't want the kids to think she was nerdy.

"Hurry up!" I said, nudging her leg with my foot.

"I'm almost done. Chill." Suddenly, pricks of heat spiked up my neck. "Chill" was one of Nia Tate's favorite words. She wasn't my favorite person.

I folded my paper in half and then in quarters, as Maddie continued to craft her perfect letters. I finished my Slurpee, and checked Maddie's to see if there was any left in hers, which, as usual, there wasn't.

"Okay," said Maddie. "I'm done."

She folded her paper and turned it into an origami bird. "I bet you put Mr. Roma first."

"How did you guess? He's soooo hot. I love his bushy mustache." Mr. Roma is the head custodian, and he loves to sing heavy metal–type songs when he mops. "All right," she said. "Let's read each other's list, one at a time."

"Okay," I said.

She raised her eyebrows up and down. "I'm reading yours first."

I shook my head. "No way!"

"Okay, fine. Be a wimp. Here." She tossed me her list/perfect-looking crane.

"It's sooo cute. I feel bad about ruining it."

Maddie shrugged. "It's okay, Soph. I'll make you another one just like it, with real origami paper."

"Okay, in that case . . ." I tore open the bird so I could read Maddie's list.

MADDIE'S HOT LIST

1) Auggie Martin
2) Tyler Finkel
3) Nick Hyde
4) Bear Arvanites
5) Matt James

"Aha!" I yelled. "Square pulled in the number one spot." Square was our special code name for Auggie because he had kind of a big, square-shaped head. "I knew you still liked him!" She had been crushing on him for a solid year, although she claimed to be over her Auggie phase.

Maddie shrugged apologetically. "I just couldn't put anyone else as number one. It's his freckles." She tapped her own freckles on her nose. "It means we're connected."

"But what's up with Tyler?" I asked. "He loves to talk. I thought you didn't like chatty guys."

"I don't. But he's kind of funny." Then Maddie motioned at me. "Okay, your turn," said Maddie. "Hand it over."

I reluctantly tossed over the hot list.

Maddie smiled so her brown eyes crinkled, then she gazed down at my list. Suddenly, she peeped her eyes over the edge of the paper. "Of course, Hayden's first."

"Blue," I corrected. Blue was our special code name for Hayden.

As if my dad had an antenna for something private going on, I heard him clomping down the hall, back from his bike ride. I quickly grabbed the lists and sparkly pen and stuck them in my pocket. Before I could sit down, he peeked his head into my bedroom. "Hi, girls."

"Hi, Mr. Fanuchi!" said Maddie.

Stretching his arm behind his head, I noticed how

baggy Dad's shirt looked. That was because he'd been working out a lot ever since he started dating a bunch. "So what's going on, you two?" he asked.

"Nothing," I said.

"Nothing?" His gaze wandered down to the red truth M&M's. "Nothing. I see." Dad grinned. "Well, nothing looks like fun. And since you're busy doing nothing, Soph, would you walk Rusty. Remember? I'm going out for lunch."

Ugh. He was going out on a date with Mrs. Tate, who worked as a math teacher at our school and happened to be the mom of Nia, the CEO of the popular group.

I was about to say, *Do I have to?*, when I heard the hot lists in my pocket making a crinkling sound. I had to get those lists out of my house and destroyed. My dad is a very nosy person and has been known to inspect my garbage.

"Okay, we'll walk Rusty! I'll get his leash." I grabbed Maddie's hand and pulled her up, eager to get out of the room and far away from the house. "We really do need fresh air."

Maddie's eyebrows shot up in a questioning look, while Dad smiled. "I'm liking your attitude," he said. Now that I was a seventh grader, Dad loved to talk about my attitude. Either he liked it or he felt the need to compliment me on it.

"Be back in forty-five minutes," continued Dad. "Before I leave to go on my date."

"Sure," I said, continuing to hold Maddie's hand as we tore down the hall and out of the house. We hadn't gotten too far down the block when I realized that Maddie wasn't keeping up the pace. After Rusty and I leaped over a stream of water from my neighbor's sprinkler, I turned back to Maddie. "C'mon, jump!"

But Maddie stood completely still, staring at a text message on her phone.

It had to be Heather Lopez or Nicole Eisenberg. We ate lunch with them five out of five, but on weekends, they did their thing and we did ours. "Is it Heather or Nicole?" I asked.

Maddie shook her head. "Nia."

Nia? Ugh. My stomach dipped. I knew Maddie and Nia were both taking a watercolor class at the community center, but I never pictured Nia as friendship material. She led the *aren't-I-cool* girl group, while Maddie always hung with me. I could tell Maddie that my dad, who happened to be the principal of Travis Middle School— our school—was getting ready to go out on his second date with Nia's mom. But I was sure it was going to be as unserious as the rest of the women he'd dated since Mom died when I was three.

"So, since when are you and Nia, like, texting?" I asked, keeping my voice light.

Maddie shrugged. "I dunno, just recently," and continued to keep her eyes on the screen, as if she'd just received a free pass to go to Disney World. Then she smiled really big at something she was reading.

"What?" I asked as Rusty tugged the leash and barked at a squirrel scurrying across the street.

"Oh, Nia's doing crazy stuff."

"Like?

"Making random videos with Ava and McKenzie." I didn't see how making videos was that crazy, but, then again, Nia loved to make everything she did seem crazy and superexciting. Would Maddie describe what we did together as crazy? Like going through last year's sixth-grade yearbook and color-coding everyone's photos by how nice they were? Or guzzling Slurpees, reading magazines, or watching YouTube?

Probably not.

I could feel my face going into meltdown mode. I began rubbing Rusty around the ears so Maddie couldn't tell I was upset.

"Nia wants me to come over," Maddie said, as she texted something back.

Great. Nia lived only about six blocks away, over on

Cullen Court, in a ranch house with landscaping that she described as the natural look, but really just had a ton of weeds that desperately needed to be pulled.

"Does she know you're with me?" I asked as Rusty sniffed a bush.

"It's fine, Sophie," said Maddie. "We can both go over."

"Nah." I picked a red berry off a bush that was probably poisonous and started juicing it between my fingers. The inside was all waxy looking. "It'd be weird," I said. Really, I hated the idea of being Maddie's tagalong.

"Oh, c'mon. Sophie, it'll be fun." Maddie's phone *bing*ed as a new message came in. "Nia wants me to be in the next video!" As she excitedly grabbed my arm, the berry I'd been holding dropped from my stained finger. Rusty lunged to eat it off the sidewalk, so I yanked him away. "Leave it!" I yelled. Then I turned to Maddie. "Nia only wants you in her video because they need your techie brain."

Maddie's lips clamped shut, and her freckled nose twinged. When she did that, she looked just like her mom, who's from Ireland, although Maddie's definitely a blend of both her Irish mom and her Japanese dad.

"Oh, I didn't mean it like that." Searching for a way out of that blunder, I blurted, "I just get upset when Rusty tries to eat stuff that could make him sick." Worst case scenario—he'd throw up dog chow all over me.

"That was evil." Maddie held up one finger.

"Sorry," I said, inwardly shuddering at Maddie using a Nia expression.

Maddie pushed up her lavender glasses. "You don't think it's possible for Nia and all of them to actually like me?"

"Sure, but . . ." I sighed. Actually, I didn't. Maddie tried too hard and was considered geeky by Nia's hippie-chic standards of cool. Plus, you had to have long, flowy hair. Maddie's dark brown hair was straight and chin-length.

"You're so good at computer-type stuff," I told Maddie. "And maybe, yeah, they need editing help." Everything I said was coming out wrong, and, at that very moment, I could feel Maddie slipping away from me. Who would tell her when assignments were due? Who would be there for post-bedtime texting discussions about what wear to school the next day? It couldn't be Nia.

I had to do something. "Look, the real reason, I don't want to go over is"—I lowered my voice and prayed for a decent idea—"I've got something planned."

"Like?"

"It's really crazy."

"What?"

My eyes flicked over at the middle school, which was

a half-block away. "Something over there." Nothing was coming to me yet, but I figured the school had possibilities.

Looking confused, Maddie stared blankly at the empty parking lot. "Travis?"

"Yep." I spied one of those blind-your-eyes bright drama club posters flapping on the door to the gym and went with it. "It's open. For rehearsals of those comedy one-acts. Dad told me he was going to check to see how things were going with the plays when he went out on his run."

"What's up?"

"Well . . ." My hands went into my pocket. Impulsively, I pulled out the folded-up hot lists. "It involves these. And . . ." I whipped out the sparkly pen that we had used to write up the hot lists. "This! And you'll just have to find out!" I charged down the sidewalk, with Rusty at my heels, hoping that jogging would give me time to think of what I'd actually do. I wished a brilliant thought would pop into my brain like popcorn.

But no ideas popped. Rusty was pulling too hard on the leash, and Maddie was screaming after me, "Stop!"

Jogging backward, I waved the hot lists over my head. "You'll have to catch up!"

It felt good to run, even though it was boiling outside, and there was hardly any shade. Most of the trees had been planted when our subdivision was built, about five years ago.

I'm a much faster runner than Maddie. First of all, even though Maddie's superskinny, I'm in better shape because of being on the soccer team, and my legs are way longer, so it wasn't hard to get a huge lead on her. The most exercise Maddie ever got was turning the page of a romance novel.

Maddie might have had a chance, but a lady in her minivan was pulling out of the driveway. I jogged in place as I waited for the van to finish backing out. Then I crossed the street, and raced over to the bike rack in front of the school to tie up Rusty. Dad, the principal, would kill me if I brought him inside the school.

When Maddie got to the bike rack, she bent over, catching her breath. "Hold up!" she said. "I just have to tell Nia what I'm doing."

"You better not."

"I mean, I'll tell her I'm busy and can't come over right now." She smiled at me. "Doing something mysterious, inside of Travis."

Yes, I thought, *score one for me!*

But then reality set in. What was I doing?

I still wasn't exactly sure myself. But I sure felt good about Maddie texting Nia that she wasn't coming over.

After I carefully opened and closed the door to the school, so it wouldn't alert anyone that we were inside, I motioned for Maddie to follow me down the hall.

"What are we doing?" she asked.

"You'll see," I said in my most ultra wait-and-see voice. It felt good to play it up like that. Honestly, I'm the best person I know at keeping secrets. But I was keeping the answer a secret, even from myself.

As I surveyed the hallway, my heart thumped loudly. Everything looked normal. Long rolls of blue paper had been tacked up on the walls, announcing an exciting visit for next week of an author who would open the door to reading. Nobody seemed to be around. Still, I didn't like the idea of being so exposed. Right now I wanted a closed door.

That's when I heard someone or something banging down the hall. We both hid around the corner. I peeked out to see Squid Rodriquez, in his red ski hat and neon, glow-in-the-dark green soccer shoes, doing cartwheels and belting out an off-key tune to himself, at the far end of the hall. "He must be here to rehearse," I whispered. "Wherever he is, we need to be somewhere else."

"Uh-huh," said Maddie, who quickly turned away from me—probably busy texting Nia. Squid had been annoying people for as long as I could remember. Not only was he the shortest guy in the seventh grade, he was also the noisiest and weirdest. I mean, who but he would bring chocolate-covered grasshoppers in his lunch for dessert, juggle them in the air, and eat them?

I needed to go someplace private. Where could I go? Then I thought of the perfect place. I pointed to the girls' bathroom. "In there."

"The bathroom?" Maddie did her forehead wrinkle. "What's in here?" she asked, following me in. I could see her taking in the faucets with the usual drip, the salmon pink–tiled walls with some faint permanent Sharpie marks. She gave me another baffled look. "Soph, I don't get it."

I didn't get it myself, which made me upset. "Shhh!" I put my fingers to my lips. "Somebody could be inside." I crouched down to see if there were feet in any of the stalls. I'm kind of shoe-obsessed and can recognize half our class by the shoes they wear. "Nobody. Good. We can talk."

"Oka-ay. Will you *finally* tell me what's going on?"

Darting around, my eyes latched on that poem about Mr. Pan, the gym teacher, that someone wrote on the wall, then, suddenly—faster than you can flush a note down a toilet—I had it. The great, big, fun idea I was looking for catapulted inside my head.

"This!" I waved the sparkly pen and the hot lists. I felt a little bit like a fraud to be so dramatic and important-sounding, like I was being Nia or something, but it was working. Maddie gazed at me, as if I was the preview to the *Avatar* sequel. "Watch," I announced. "And be amazed."

I pushed opened the end stall, which was more spacious and had an opaque window with a ledge we could lean against. "C'mon," I said, motioning to Maddie. We crammed into the stall, closing the door and giggling. I then wrote on the back of the door, in all caps, THE HOT LIST.

"You are craaaa-zy!" sang out Maddie, putting her phone away in her back pocket.

Excitement bubbles filled my chest, a few of them popping under the weight of a little fear. "Shhh. Not so loud!"

"This is so messed-up." Maggie giggled.

"Yup." Thank goodness my dad was at home, getting ready for his date. If he saw me in this bathroom, writing on the back of this door, he would not be happy. I smiled. "Watch! I'm going to combine your list with mine, and create one uberlist." I held up both lists in one hand as I wrote.

"Whoa," said Maddie. "Your dad will kill you if he finds out."

Yeah, I'd second that. How I wish I'd had a different

idea, like making confetti out of those hot lists and flushing them down the toilet!

But nooooooo, I had to have that one genius idea in order to get Maddie's attention. I mean, in the pit of my stomach, I knew it was bad. Like wearing-pajamas-to-class-to-start-a-new-fashion-trend bad. I mean, what was I thinking?—announcing to the world who was hot and who wasn't. That might have been texty-bloggy material for someone like Nia and her crew, but I should've known better—those lists were meant to be secret. Instead, I ignored my flip-floppy, squeezy-icky feeling inside and kept on writing.

"Guard the door," I whispered to Maddie. At least I had the sense to be paranoid about someone catching me. What I should've been paying attention to was who was about to be leaving my life for good.

Chapter Two

Maddie pulled on my elbow. *"Let me write."*

I couldn't help smiling. Maddie was getting excited about *our* Hot List. Still, I couldn't risk Maddie using the pen. "Everyone knows your handwriting. Sorry. Who else in the school does calligraphy?"

She shrugged. "Probably no one, except Madame Kearns. And not very well."

"Exactly. That's why I'm doing all caps, so no one will ever know our identities."

"But who's going to go first? Hayden—"

"Blue," I corrected, reminding her once again to use our special code name for him. Blue because of his sea-blue eyes. Blue because that's how I felt when I couldn't see Hayden in English and social studies (he was ONLY in French, gym, math, and homeroom with me). Blue because he always wore blue jeans, but regular color shirts

17

and shoes and stuff. He pretty much epitomized cool. He didn't go around speaking a ton. Kind of like me, only he fell into the extremely cool category, and I was semicool—the sporty girl who wasn't part of a big group. A one-best-friend kind of person.

And Maddie was my best friend since fourth grade. We had done everything together. In fourth grade, we raked paths through the woods behind Maddie's house and pretended they were for escaping vampires. In fifth grade, we jumped on our trampoline for gazillions of hours, and made little obstacle courses for Rusty when he was a puppy. Last year, in sixth grade, we survived getting our candy snatched by a couple of punk kids while trick-or-treating, and Maddie recorded me singing my favorite song, using GarageBand. And so far, seventh grade has been much better than everyone says.

Maddie's older sister, Gwen, swore that seventh grade was the worst year in middle school because everyone changes and gets all moody—swapping friends as easily as trading Silly Bandz. I was glad to know that because I, for one, didn't plan on changing. I liked things exactly as they were.

"You know, you really should say something to Blue," said Maddie. "About liking him."

"I don't think so."

"You could drop a hint, like carrying Blue's lacrosse stick for him." Maddie smiled. Hayden was famous for carrying his lacrosse stick everywhere he went, even now, when it wasn't lacrosse season.

"Yeah, right," I said again, as my stomach bunched up.

"I bet he'd like you. You're so pretty."

"Yeah, sure," I said, running my fingers through my hair, which is probably my best feature. It's long and dark brown and essentially frizz-free. My eyes are hazel, which means they're neither green nor brown, like they can't make up their mind. I guess, if I were to start wearing more makeup, I could glam myself up more, but that's not me. I'm more of a lip-gloss-and-a-touch-of-mascara kind of girl.

"Okay, we need to decide who's going to go first," I said, irritated that Maddie had pulled out her phone again to check for her new messages. "Blue or Square?"

"Square," said Maddie, putting up her thumb for her crush, Auggie.

"Definitely Blue," I said, thinking that Hayden just had to be number one.

"I've got a coin!" Maddie pulled a penny out of her pocket, and we flipped for it. I picked tails and won.

As I jotted down Hayden's name at the top of the List, I thought the sparkly ink looked extra sparkly. Softly, I hummed the tune to this new song that I really liked.

"Let me write. I can do caps too." Maddie got that frowny look again.

I continued to hum and ignored Maddie's pleas because I was afraid she'd make even her caps look, somehow, like calligraphy.

"C'mon," she begged.

I sang a little louder this time, actually singing the lyrics instead of just humming along to the tune.

"Sophie, you're *such* a good singer," gushed Maddie. "You could be professional."

I stopped singing. "Yeah, right." When I'm by myself I love to sing, but I can't sing in front of people at all. Well, except for Maddie, my dad, and Rusty. And what's a dog going to say about my singing?

"It's true," said Maddie. "You're the best. You have to sing at the school talent show. I think it's in December; that's three short months." The talent show was a fund-raiser for leadership, and it was a huge deal.

"Yeah. Like that's ever going to happen. Can you imagine me on stage? Never!"

"I don't get it. You play soccer in front of people."

"That's different. You look at the ball, not the people watching the ball."

"Okay, I'm just sayin'," said Maddie. "You're really

good. Ah, c'mon now, give me the pen. Please? Please?"

"All right," I conceded. "Fine. Go ahead. But in all caps!" As I handed her the lists, I noticed that her list ran a little longer down the page than mine, because she had added a name on the bottom and then crossed it off. I hadn't noticed that before. "Who did you cross out?" I asked.

"No one. I just misspelled a name, and rewrote it."

"Oh, just wondering." I handed Maddie the pen, and she finished writing up the list, alternating between the guys on her list and mine. And then, because our list didn't seem long enough, we added other guys until we had twenty total.

Suddenly, Maddie's eyes started twinkling. "I think we should add girls, too."

"Girls?"

"It's not just boys who are hot." She shook her hips. "I'm hot! And you, too!"

"Hey, I'm not going to stop you. Go for it."

Then, next to the guys' Hot List, she started creating a girls' Hot List and writing in girls' names. When I saw the first name that she wrote, I inwardly groaned. Nia, of course.

"She has the best hair in the school," said Maddie.

It was true. Nia had these Taylor Swift, golden blond

curls. She added the rest of Nia's long-haired, flowy posse—Ava, McKenzie, Amber, and Sierra. And then her eyes gleamed. "Now I'm going to put me and you on the Hot List."

"No," I said, grabbing the pen away from her. "Don't you dare."

"Why not?"

I could hear an adult calling down the hall to someone, so I lowered my voice. "Because if we put our names, and anyone happens to see it, they'll know we wrote it. C'mon. Let's be serious. We're not Hot List material."

"That's not true," said Maddie. "You're so pretty." She glanced at my long, jean capri–clad legs. "And you're model tall, and you'd be taller if you didn't slump."

"Thanks for sounding like my dad."

"Sorry." She bit her bottom lip. "But it's true. If I put my name on the Hot List, it'd be a dead giveaway that I wrote it." She glanced at her hoodie, which she had paired with checkered leggings and strappy sandals. I had patiently explained to her earlier in the morning that if you're going to go for casual, you've got to extend that all the way down to your footwear. But unfortunately, those were the only clothes she had packed for the sleepover.

Maddie tapped her owl-shaped lavender glasses. "These are another problem. I can't wait until I get contacts." And she looked down at her chest. "Still like a brick wall down there." She smiled up at me. "But I could put you on the List."

"Maddie, to get on the Hot List you've got to play the popularity game. Sometimes I wear any old hoodie to school. I don't do the *talk*. I'm not into the drama. Am I part of a girl clan? No. You've got to be seen as someone who's part of an inner circle. And that's just not my thing."

"Okay," she grabbed the pen back. "I don't agree with you, but whatever. What about Heather and Nicole?"

"They're fine, but *definitely* not Hot List material. They're too off on their own." I watched as Maddie slowly added a couple more seventh graders, and then a bunch of sixth graders who were really cute—Clara Pessereau, Sarah Ruinsky, and Jane Cockrell. She made her letters really perfect-looking.

"Give me the pen," I said. "We need to add some eighth-grade girls, too." So I added a bunch of girls that I knew from the soccer team until we had twenty names. The same amount as the guys. Maddie checked her phone again. "Ta-da!" I said, standing back from it.

Maddie smiled at me. "The official Hot List."

We put our arms around each other's shoulders, admiring our work. And the pure insanity of it. "I can't believe we just did this," I said.

"Me either. But it was your idea."

"You helped write it," I countered.

"Everyone's going to see this on Monday, and the whole school's going to be chatting about why Ava came before McKenzie, and wondering who likes Hayden, who likes Auggie, and then start trying to figure it all out. It will be like that time that somebody left an anonymous love note on the bleachers in gym, but they addressed it to *S* and signed it *C*."

I laughed, but my stomach started to flutter and felt queasy. "No, it won't be like that because I'm going to wipe the whole thing off with a paper towel."

Maddie twirled the pen in her fingers. "Sorry. It's a permanent marker."

"It is? Guess I kind of knew that." We both laughed.

Suddenly, I heard the click click of heels clomping toward the bathroom. "What's that?" Maddie whispered.

"Uh-oh!" I said. "Someone's coming."

I pulled the stall door shut and locked it. Then I realized that two people in a stall looked sort of weird. "There's two of us in here," I blurted. "Hurry, jump on the toilet," I panic-whispered.

Maddie gave me her you-are-so-crazy look. "No, you jump up."

As the footsteps grew louder, I hopped up on the

toilet and braced myself with my arms so I wouldn't fall in. Maddie started giggling. "Stop it," I pleaded. "They'll hear."

That's when I glanced down at Maddie's shoes. Right. She was wearing her lavender sandals. Only Maddie wore lavender sandals at Travis. It was her signature color. If whoever was about to walk into the bathroom checked out the shoes of the people in the bathroom, like I had, they'd know it was her in a second. I furiously motioned at her shoes, then for Maddie to hop up on the toilet with me, which she did.

Only, toilets aren't really big enough for two people, so there we were. I was straddling half the rim. And Maddie was straddling the other half. And we were clinging to each other so we wouldn't fall into the bowl. I had to bite down on my lip not to laugh. This was soooooo insane.

"Rehearsals took for*ever*." It sounded like it was Rose Workman, an eighth grader who was the star of every show, including last year's musical, *Footloose*, and the only girl at the school taller than me.

"I know it," said someone else in irritation. "I had to call my mom to tell her to pick me up late."

Then one of the girls clicked right over to our stall. I tried not to breathe.

"Hey, it's locked," said Irritated Girl.

"That's weird," said Rose.

Then I heard Irritated Girl open up the stall next to ours.

Maddie squeezed her eyes shut, and I silently begged, *Please don't hear us. Please, please, please.* We gave each other this look that said, *This is so messed up!*

Finally, I heard the toilet flush and Irritated Girl washed her hands, which took forever. Obviously, she was one of those germaphobes.

Then they both talked about how boring blocking the show was and to hurry because Mrs. Regis wanted to lock up. Then finally, FINALLY, they left—only Maddie and I still didn't move until we were sure that they were actually gone.

"We've got to get out of here," whispered Maddie. "We could get locked in the school for the whole weekend."

"No, wait. They could come back," I whispered back.

"Why?"

"One last look in the mirror. I don't know."

So we stayed like that for a couple more paranoid minutes until I fell and banged against the toilet paper dispenser. "Ow!" The pen flew out of my hands and clattered onto the tile. "You know we've got to throw it away. It's evidence." I stuffed it into the bottom of the trash.

"Farewell," said Maddie.

"Nice knowing you," I said. Suddenly, I felt an ache in

my chest. And it was the oddest thing, but tears sprang into my eyes. It was not like me to be all weepy. "This is crazy. It's just a pen."

But it wasn't really. As we walked out of the bathroom and down the hall, carefully avoiding anyone, I thought about how Maddie had mailed the pen as well as a journal to me from Spain. It had been perfect timing for my birthday present because I had been really feeling alone without her around during the summer. She found it in an art shop in Barcelona where her dad was doing architectural research. The journal was still sitting unopened at the bottom of my drawer.

"Uh-huh," she said, as her phone made that text *bing*y sound.

"Nia again?" I said irritably. That girl didn't give up.

Glancing at the screen, Maddie shook her head. "Nope, your dad."

"Why's he texting *you*?"

"Because you forgot your phone. Big dummy."

"Oh, right." I shrugged. I had left it in the pocket of my backpack. That was more like something Maddie would do, not me. I was definitely not myself today.

"Apparently, you're supposed to be back before he leaves for his date."

"The date." I bit my lip. "I can't believe it's already been an hour." I had promised I'd be back in forty-five minutes. "I swear, it feels like it's been fifteen minutes."

That's when we both bolted out of the school to get back to my house. "Promise not to tell anyone about this," I said as we jogged over to Rusty.

"I promise," said Maddie.

Chapter Three

As I put my books in my locker before homeroom on Monday morning, my stomach felt twisty as I thought about the Hot List. "Do you think anyone's seen it yet?" I whispered to Maddie, who was trying to close her locker.

"Seen what?"

"You know what." Beside me, Brianna Evans twirled the combination to her locker, and Trent Eckhart tossed his baseball cap into the locker next to mine. I flicked my head toward the bathroom.

"Oh, that." Maddie pushed her locker again, but it wasn't completely closing. I could see a binder sticking out of the bottom.

"Here," I shoved the binder in with the rest of her mess, then quickly kicked the door shut before an avalanche of books thundered out of the locker.

"Thanks!" said Maddie.

I shrugged. "No problem."

Out of the corner of my eye, I saw two health teachers, Mrs. Moriarity and Ms. Crenshaw, talking and glancing over at me. Mrs. Moriarity pointed at me, while Ms. Crenshaw craned forward. My heart began thumping. Did they know we wrote up the Hot List?

I nudged Maddie with my shoulder. "They're looking at us," I said.

Maddie smiled and spoke through closed teeth. "That's because of the new trophy case. Right behind you."

I whirled around. "Oh, wow. Didn't notice that." The old trophy case had been replaced with new glass, and there was even lighting at the top of the shelves so the medals and stuff gleamed. "Guess I'm getting all paranoid."

"Just a little," Maddie said as the bell for homeroom rang. "Stop worrying, Soph. See?" She pointed to the mobbed hallway, where students were rushing past us and chatting together. "Nobody's staring at you."

"Good," I said. That was *exactly* how I liked it.

Of course, when I got to homeroom, I couldn't stop Mrs. McGibbon from gazing at me and gushing in her formal tone, "Good morning, Miss Fanuchi."

"Good morning," I answered back.

I've gotten used to teachers being extra friendly to

me because I'm the principal's daughter. But it still was embarrassing. And some teachers were more obvious than others. Mrs. McGibbon was definitely a brownnoser.

"Would you like to help me staple?" Mrs. McGibbon pointed to a stack of science papers about amoebas and other single-celled organisms. I didn't really want to, but I didn't think I had a choice. When I grow up, I'll marry an insurance agent, or someone who has nothing to do with middle schools. My children shouldn't have to suffer like me.

"Sure. Yeah, I'll do it." Stapling would actually give me something to do, especially since Maddie was not in my homeroom, or anyone else I was superfriendly with, and I wouldn't have to worry about the Hot List. Anyway, Hayden happened to be in my homeroom. He sat, with his lacrosse stick at his feet, in the back of the class, playing paper football with Auggie. And I was sure, if he met my eyes, somehow, he'd just know that I wrote his name on the stall of the bathroom, as number one.

Today, he was wearing a dark blue T-shirt with a lacrosse stick logo on it that matched the color of his eyes.

Blue really was a perfect code name for him.

Except it also meant sad. And sad was the opposite of how I felt when I saw Hayden.

As I was stapling, I suddenly heard giggling, out-of-control girls. Nia, Ava, Sierra, McKenzie, and Amber were all bunched up, shoving one another and laughing in the hallway.

Then Nia stuck her head into the classroom. She had pulled her hair back with a clip but let some loose curls cascade into her face. As usual, she sported lots of layers, in all kinds of textures and colors, as well as multiple necklaces and bangles. For a moment, she glanced at me. And my heart hammered away. Oh, my god. She knew. Somehow. Some way.

"Can I help you?" asked Mrs. McGibbon, glancing at Nia. Since Nia headed seventh-grade leadership, she often was handing out official flyers about school dances and stuff.

"No, I was just checking something," said Nia. Then she flicked her eyes over at Hayden.

"Hi, Hayden!" she cooed, shaking her head so her blondish corkscrew curls bobbed. "You're number one!" Today, she had on yellow leggings, gray suede boots, a white, oversize tank top with sage green swirls, a vest, and a wide tan belt with a big peace-sign buckle.

But right now, I didn't feel like she was bringing peace. I held my breath. What could be the worst-case scenario? Answer: that Nia would call out that Hayden was number one on my personal hot list.

Hayden glanced up from his desk and grinned. Then

Ava and McKenzie, who were flanking Nia, chorused, "Number one!" and they all giggled down the hall, both their long hair and their clothes flowing.

I breathed a sigh of relief. Yay! They didn't seem to know it was *my* hot list! Huzzah!

Auggie began shoving Hayden and said in a falsetto voice. "Eww, those girls think you're number one!"

"Hayden, looks like you've got some lacrosse fans," murmured Mrs. McGibbon. She didn't seem mad that Nia hadn't been delivering official school flyers or something. Part of me wanted Mrs. McGibbon to write up Nia. But that'd be stupid. Then Nia might start talking to my dad about the Hot List.

"He's numero uno, bay-bee!" shouted Squid Rodriquez, pointing at Hayden and then waving a finger in the air. Of course, I knew they didn't mean number one in lacrosse.

They meant number one on the Hot List.

As Hayden flicked the paper football across his desk, I could see a blush spread to the tips of his ears. Wait a minute. Had he noticed Nia looking at me and then at him? Did he make a connection?

As in, did he know he was *my* number one? I pressed the heel of my hand down hard on the stapler, only my pointer finger got in the way. I felt a needle-sharp stabbing pain. "Ouch!" I yelled, and began hopping in pain.

"What's the matter?" Mrs. McGibbon dashed over to me, the crease above her nose puckering.

Bravely, I looked down at my finger. No staple. Just two holes with drops of blood.

Mrs. McGibbon handed me some tissues from a box on her desk. "Hold this over your finger. Let's get you down to the nurse."

I shook my head. "I'm fine. Seriously." Going down to the nurse meant that my dad would be called, and everyone would make a huge production out of it. Not good.

"You at least need a Band-Aid," stated Mrs. McGibbon.

Brianna Evans, who was always the first to know the gossip, flew to my side. "Ow!" she pressed her fingers to her mouth like she was the one who had been hurt. She gazed at Bear Arvanites, who she constantly flirted with. They were always pushing, shoving, and generally maiming each other. "Bear, would you like to me to staple your finger?" she asked teasingly.

"Staple yourself," growled Bear, whose real name was William, but Bear fit him much better since he was big and fuzzy-haired.

"Does it hurt?" she asked.

"The staple didn't actually go in. See?" I showed Brianna the little bubble of blood. "I'm fine," I said.

"I hate blood," said Brianna, moaning and turning her head away.

Auggie and Hayden craned their necks to get a better look. Hayden probably thought I was a complete stapling idiot. And naturally, Squid stood on his chair to get a better view. "Would you like me to call up Spider-Man or get the Green Hornet to save you?" asked Squid.

"Enough!" said Mrs. McGibbon. "Focus on your prep work, everyone."

Mrs. McGibbon inspected my finger. "Have you had a tetanus shot recently?"

I nodded. "During the summer."

"Good. Let me get you a Band-Aid." She reached up onto a shelf and pulled out a red first-aid box, and insisted on putting on antibiotic cream first and then the Band-Aid. I liked looking at her long nails, which she painted burgundy. Would I ever grow long nails like that? Probably not, since I bit them all of the time.

As the bell rang, I went back to pick up my backpack.

At that moment, Hayden brushed past me, but he slowed down. "You okay?"

"Yeah," I said, even though my finger was now kind of throbbing. But suddenly, I didn't really mind. My hurt finger was the reason for my first conversation with Hayden. I tried to think of something more to add about my finger, but my mouth went in reverse. I also found it really hard to look him in those sea-blue eyes. But I did check out his footwear. He was sporting a new pair of red Vans.

"See ya," said Hayden with a grin as he caught up with Auggie. *See you,* as in he was happy about the idea of looking at me again. And he asked if I was okay, which meant I occupied space in his brain. I couldn't wait to tell Maddie. But I didn't really have the chance. Hot List hysteria was sweeping the school by first period.

Chapter Four

Texts sent and received on Sophie Fanuchi's phone:

    First Period

    Travis Middle School

    Boulder, Colorado

    USA

    Monday, September 7

    Between 8:27 a.m. and 8:31 a.m.

    Central Time

Sophiegrl *8:27 AM* September 7

ppl have gon epic crzy. Kip calm

Laughfactor *8:29 AM* September 7

Hot List =P

Sophiegrl *8:30 AM* September 7

yeah <

In the hallway outside of Mrs. Tate's first period math class, Squid bounced around and tapped his T-shirt, which pictured a flying sandwich and the words I NEED A HERO.

"If there's a hot list," said Squid, "I know I'm on it. Oh, yeah, bay-bee! The digs chick me!" *The digs chick me* was Squid's dumb little personal saying he made up. He swiveled his hips and danced around like he was stepping on burning coals. A couple of girls started laughing at him. And Auggie and a bunch of his baseball friends rolled their eyes.

Maddie smiled at me knowing that Squid wasn't on the List, unless it was a list for weird boys in shirts featuring baloney sandwiches who thought they were funny when they were lame instead. Immediately I stared at the tiles on the floor, so I didn't start cracking up.

At that moment, Nia swept down the hallway, and I watched her long corkscrew curls bounce up and down. "Sorry, Squid," she said, snapping one of the elastic hair bands on her wrist. She always wore at least twenty in different colors. It was part of her fashion statement, I guess. Or maybe she just liked being the human ponytail holder. "Dude—you're not on *the* List."

Then she looked at me for a moment and sort of half-smiled. "But I am." And she glanced back at her friends. "And they are too." She played with the New Agey crystal pendant on her leather cord choker-necklace.

"Which means you're officially not hot," added one of her posse, Ava, in her breathy, scowly voice. She was always acting mad about something, and Nia was constantly whisking her away to comfort her. Usually I had no idea what Ava actually had to be mad about. She was tall and slender, with gorgeous almond-colored skin and hair, and she held her body perfectly straight like she was riding a horse, which she did on the weekends and won major horse awards for.

"If I'm not on the List," said Squid, contorting his face, "that's 'cause you wrote it." He dug some change out of his pockets. "I'll pay you to put me on the List."

"That's so sad," said Nia, tipping her head forward and transferring one of the hair bands off her wrist into her hair to make a ponytail. "But I didn't write anee-thing. The List just appeared," she said dramatically. "It just is."

"It just is," repeated McKenzie, another posse member, in the same sort of whispery magic-sounding voice. McKenzie always spoke barely above a whisper. She made me seem talkative and loud. "And it's amazingly accurate," she continued.

This was *too* weird. It was like they thought the List had magical powers, as if it were animated. I watched Nia and her groupies strut to their seats, so I could hang back a minute with Maddie.

"Can you believe them?" I whispered to Maddie.

"I know," she said, pushing up her glasses. She glanced around and then whispered, "Everyone's talking about our list!" She smiled so hard I thought her cheeks would pop. "Even Square." Auggie, aka Square, who lived down the block from Maddie, was always out in the front yard pitching a baseball against a net. Maddie really felt sorry for him, since it appeared that he didn't have anyone to play catch with, except for the net, of course. So, in July she had offered to throw with him. After a couple of tosses together, he said he'd rather play with the net. Ouch.

Maddie got the hint that he liked his net better than her, but she definitely still thought Auggie was cute. Which he was, I guess, in a lonely, throwing-a-baseball-by-yourself-in-front-of-the-house-for-hours kind of way. I never understood why he didn't practice pitching in the backyard, where no one could see him being by himself. I would never expose my lack of friends like that. Maybe I'm paranoid—and I guess I am—because a scary thought hit me.

I leaned into Maddie, whispering, "What if Blue or Square figure out it was us?"

"How?" asked Maddie.

"Like if the ink from the pen started appearing on my hands or something."

"You threw away the pen, remember?"

"So? Stuff like that happens in horror movies."

Maddie laughed. "This is *real* life."

"Yeah, I guess." I remembered Maddie's sister, Gwen, telling us last summer that middle school was like living an actual horror movie. "Full of hapless victims who have no idea of what lurks around the corner," she said. I guess that's how they talk in college. They use words like "hapless." I made Maddie remind me never to go around sounding like a term paper when I get that old.

Maddie tucked her chin-length hair behind her ears. "It's kind of cool. It's like we're famous, but only we know it. Like one of those authors with a pen name. Get it? A pen name."

"I get it," I said, smiling.

Mrs. Tate stood up behind her desk. "C'mon in, ya'll. Sit down," she said, looking at the students standing in the doorway. Mrs. Tate was from Virginia and had a definite Southern accent. She peered over at me. "Sophie, Maddie. That means y'all, too."

As Maddie and I sat down, I thought about how Mrs. Tate was one of the few teachers who was really good about not being all gushy over me because I was the principal's kid. But, of course, she was dating my dad. I guess she was gushy about him. When Mrs. Tate had us do individual work, I stole some secret glances at her.

WHAT WAS SPECIAL ABOUT MRS. TATE TO MAKE HER DATEABLE

1. She was from Virginia and had a cute Southern accent. Nia didn't have the accent, except when she wanted to cut someone in line. Otherwise, she sounded like everyone else in Boulder.

2. Mrs. Tate was really pretty but didn't wear makeup, which made her look natural. Like, you could imagine her as the mom in an ad for organic yogurt.

3. My dad could practice his Southern accent on her, since he liked to try on all kinds of dialects. I guess he thought it was amusing.

Which it was—sometimes—when it wasn't annoying.

During the rest of class, everybody was secretly checking their phones and passing notes and chatting about the Hot List. I even got texts from Heather and Nicole asking if I had checked out the Hot List yet.

That was like asking Thomas Edison if he'd heard of the light bulb.

Or the Wright Brothers if they knew what an airplane was.

Or Samuel Morse whether he'd heard of Morse code. Not to beat a dead horse but . . .

Did I ever know about the Hot List? Hello! I invented it.

Later in the day, at the beginning of lunch, there was an actual line outside the girls' bathroom, next to the band room, to get in to see the Hot List.

"This is madness," I said to Maddie. They were all swarming like bees outside a hive because of me, Sophie. Or, as they say in Madame Kearn's French class, *moi!* "Do you really think they're all there just because of the Hot List? Like, maybe some of them really do need to brush their teeth or something?"

Maddie gave me a *what-are-you-crazy?* look.

Electrical currents zapped through the air, and every spark had to do with the List. Pride filled my chest. Maddie and I both slowed by the line outside the bathroom to listen in on snippets of conversation:

"I heard that Auggie is number one."

"Sorry, it's Hayden."

"Nia was number one for the girls."

"Is it only for seventh graders?" asked a boy who was passing by.

"I think so," someone else replied. "But there are sixth-graders on there. And eighth graders, so it's hard to say."

"I heard the List glows in the dark."

"I heard it's invisible ink, which will disappear at midnight."

"Does anyone know who wrote it?" asked a girl wearing tie-dyed tights.

"No, it's a big mystery," said another girl with a hoodie that almost covered her eyes.

Of course, only Maddie and I knew the answer to that puzzle, and we weren't talking. I felt seriously happy.

Maddie was right. It felt like being famous without anyone even knowing. I was also glad that Maddie didn't seem focused on Nia. With the Hot List, I had found the missing key to locking in our friendship.

At lunch everyone kept on going over to the Hot

Listers and making all kinds of jokes. Like "Ouch!" and "Too hot to touch."

I must have seen at least a half dozen people pretend to burn their hands on Nia, including Brianna Evans, Squid Rodriquez, and some girls I played with on the soccer team.

Of course, the same thing was happening to the rest of the Listers, even by other Hot Listers. I watched Sierra touch fingers with Nia and heard them yell together "Hot List power!" and then blow on their fingers, like they were extinguishing flames.

And I watched McKenzie and Ava throw ice on Hayden and yell, "Maybe this will cool you down now." And then Hayden did the same back to them.

I wondered if I were on the Hot List, would Hayden do the same with me?

Seeing him get all of that attention from the girls in Nia's group made me a little nervous. As we went to sit at our usual table with Heather and Nicole, I whispered to Maddie, "Now everyone will start to like Blue. He isn't just my secret anymore."

"Oh, get over yourself," Maddie whispered back. "He's supercute. I bet that if he found out that you put him as number one, he'd ask you to slow dance at Winterfest, for sure."

I thwacked her on the shoulder. "Stop it!" I said as

we sat down to eat. I couldn't imagine anything more embarrassing than Hayden actually knowing that I liked him. But Maddie kept making goo-goo eyes at me and silently mouthing, *Blue*.

"Stop it!" I repeated.

"Stop what?" asked Heather, as she held up her tuna sandwich and narrowed her eyes.

Maddie flicked a quick glance at me and then said, "Oh, she wants me to stop talking about the Hot List."

"Who needs it," I said dramatically.

"And I can actually see two Hot Listers' heads swelling right now," said Nicole in her usual lightning-fast way of speaking. "I agree. It's annoying."

I had considered telling Heather and Nicole that we were the ones who started the Hot List. But we weren't really close, in the sharing-your-deepest-darkest-secret kind of way. I guess we all had a friendship of convenience. We were more like two sets of best friends that ate together versus an official group.

"The whole school's whispering about the Hot List, don't you think?" said Heather, who always spoke like she was asking a question.

"I saw Teddy combing his hair, like, ten hundred times," Nicole said, "between third and fourth. And he made it look flat."

"Uh-oh," said Heather. "Flat hair. He'll get knocked off the List. Someone should warn him, right? The Listmaker might see."

The Listmaker? Wow. That was us. Maddie and I glanced at each other, trying not to give ourselves away. It was really hard not to burst into giggles.

"I even overheard Maura Hogenhuis in the hallway saying maybe she should dump Brad Jeffries since he wasn't on the Hot List," said Nicole. "Can you believe it?"

I couldn't. Someone wanted to get rid of an actual boyfriend because he didn't make it onto my list or Maddie's? It was just a list. Written in a bathroom. How much credit could you really give it?

Apparently lots.

In my head I wondered what other kinds of lists I could create. The food list? Like if I put mushrooms as my favorite food, would everyone start packing hydrated fungi for lunch?

Or the friend list, which would name the girls who are best friend material. Would those ten girls get friends and nobody else?

Or the color list? If Maddie put her favorite color as purple, would the whole school start dressing in shades of it?

Probably. Through lists, it'd be so easy to become the

invisible dictator of Travis Middle School. Tempting.

After the bell rang for fifth period, a clump of eighth-grade girls passed by us in the hallway. I watched one of them show her friend a photo of the Hot List on her phone.

"Whoa!" Maddie needled me with her elbow. "Looks like it's going to be posted everywhere soon. Soph, we're going to be seriously famous." Maddie hustled down the hallway, only her backpack wasn't quite zipped, so a couple of books tumbled out and crashed to the floor.

"Hold up!" I said. "Your books."

I helped Maddie pick them up and secured them in her backpack.

"Thanks," she said. "You're the best."

"No, you're the best."

"No, you."

"NO, YOU!" And then we both burst out laughing.

I cupped my hands and whispered something into Maddie's ear: "We've got a secret."

"We do," said Maddie, giggling.

And we just looked at each other, smiling and knowing that there was just one other person on the entire planet who also knew something that everyone was talking about, and that someone was your very best friend.

Chapter Five

The next day something weird happened. During lunch, Nia waltzed over to Maddie and then asked if she'd like to eat with her group. I mean, I realized that Nia and Maddie had become texting buddies ever since they took that art class, but their semifriendship never really spilled over into the actual school day too much.

But this felt different. Nia, hippie-chic queen, was publicly asking her to sit at her table, which was a big deal. And she didn't just ask, but insisted, like if Maddie didn't, the school would collapse or something.

It happened as we were heading to our usual lunch table, which was near the serving line. Nia swooped down on us, swept her long, corkscrew blond curls out of her face, and grabbed Maddie's arm. "You've got to eat with us today!"

Maddie blinked and pushed her glasses up on her nose. "What about Sophie?" she asked.

"Sophie too. Definitely."

I didn't like being an afterthought. "What about Heather and Nicole?" I mouthed.

Maddie smiled at me weakly, "It's fine," she said. "They'll understand."

I wasn't so sure that they would. But I could see Maddie's huge grin as she glanced at Nia's table, which was on the other side of the cafeteria next to the bank of windows facing the courtyard.

That's what everyone called it: Nia's table. I guess it would now be now known as the Hot List table since the entire clan (Nia, Ava, McKenzie, Sierra, and Amber) had gotten onto the Hot List. The group pretty much did EVERYTHING together. Like, right now, they were hugging and jumping and gushing about something. Probably waiting to see what kind of thing Nia would organize, like the next school dance, paint-a-mural day, or rescue un-clan girls and lasso them into their table. Even though she'd been a student at Travis for only a year, Nia was easily elected head of seventh-grade leadership, which was sort of like student council and seventh-grade class president combined into one major power trip. After going with her mom to Sedona for some kind of a purification weekend, she'd tried to convince my dad that the caf should be serving only raw foods, and they actually did it for one day.

"Hurry, let's get out of here," said Nia, glancing at the lunch line. "The smell. Ewww." Plugging her nose, she waved one hand in front of her face. "The scary, scary smell."

"You mean, the meat loaf?" I asked, glancing at someone's tray as they passed by us.

"Exactly," said Nia. "It's going to putrefy. It's red meat. From a factory where cows are lame and live squished together butt to mouth."

"Yuck," said Maddie. Nia was a very vocal vegetarian (a "Triple *V*"), and made anyone else who didn't follow the way of the carrot feel a little guilty or, in this case, grossed out.

As she dragged Maddie through the crowded lunch-room, with me following, it was like watching the parting of the Red Sea.

"Step aside," Nia cracked. Groups of guys, who were aiming their mashed-up napkins into the trash, jumped out of the way, and a clump of band girls held their trays of food up over their heads to protect Nia from the harmful effects of being too close to dead animal food. "It's Nia, the number one hottie," I heard someone call out.

Okay, it was weird to be publicly seen with Nia. But it didn't suck. I mean, Nia definitely had the queen bee thing down.

Maddie turned back to give me a look, like *Isn't it great that Nia's asking us to eat with her?*

But I pretended not to notice. Instead, I couldn't help glancing at Squid as he shouted, "Look at me!" and stuck French fries up his nose.

As we continued to follow Nia across the room, I noticed that she was more developed than the rest of us up top and carried herself like a dancer, never slumpy like me. (Sorry, but it's freaky to stand up straight when you're five inches taller than everyone, especially the boys.)

"Move, girls! Move!" Nia ordered, as she shoved our two seats into a maximally crowded table. "Say hi to Sophie and Maddie."

Some of the girls, including Amber and Sierra, did little half waves and McKenzie and Ava nodded. Maddie stared at her sandwich and grinned, like she was Dorothy arriving in Oz. Why did everyone decide that being part of the clan at Nia's table meant you were popular? "Exclusive" was more like it—Hot List exclusive. Mostly I thought it was dumb, even if part of me had occasionally fantasized about being at this table.

As we sat down, most everyone at the table was having

a conversation about how annoying this new song was on the radio.

Nia demonstrated the song by singing it extra badly. And then someone said, "Thank you."

And everyone replied, "You're welcome" at the same time and then cracked up.

"Why don't you sing it for us, Sophie?" suggested Maddie. She turned to the others at the table. "She's got an awesome voice."

I shrugged. "It's okay."

Nia peered at me knowingly. "C'mon, Sophie. Do it. You can sing badly. It's the point."

"Nah, it's okay. You do it so well." Then I clapped my hand on my mouth. "That came out wrong. I didn't mean you sing badly. I mean you sing badly on purpose well."

"We get what you meant," said Ava in an *I'm-so-over-you* voice.

Then Nia went back to singing, and I noticed that Maddie was laughing superhard, along with the rest of the girls. It wasn't that funny. Really. The whole thing was kind of dumb, and I couldn't help feeling bad about saying that Nia was a bad singer. Even if she was.

Then they started to talk about the Hot List. I didn't know if it was my imagination but they seemed to be smiling and giving Maddie and me lots of eye contact. *I am paranoid,* I thought.

"It's weird," said Nia, cutting her vegetarian burrito. "Don't you think? It's so weird. All the guys on the Hot List really and truly are the hottest."

"And girls, too," said Amber, smiling smugly.

"The List knows," said Nia.

"Totally," said Sierra. "It's weird."

"Like, if the List had come out last week," said Nia. "Auggie would have never gotten on. I mean too many"—she squinched her nose—"freckles. But something happened to him over the weekend. He really is cute. The way he struts and stuff."

"Yeah, even his voice is hot," said Amber.

"It's so sad how some of the guys think they can suddenly get onto the List. They should accept what they are and not try so hard. Like Squid. It's so sad," said Nia.

It was sooo hard not to raise my eyebrow and look knowingly at Maddie. I tried to glance at her to give a quick little secret look, but her eyes were trained on Nia.

Nia, you are being ridiculous, I wanted to say. *The List is not magic.* But I didn't want to draw attention to myself, especially as my dad, who sometimes did lunch patrol, was approaching our table.

Dad smiled extra big when he saw that I was sitting

with Nia and her crew. Not because she was popular but because he had been hinting around that it would be nice for us to get together. I heard him say it on the phone to Mrs. Tate. Now he was going to get the wrong impression, like we were friends, which meant he'd be expecting me to be friendly and maybe invite her over to our house for a sleepover. Ugh.

I really didn't want him coming over to table and asking questions. But Maddie raised her hand. "Hi, Mr. Fanuchi!"

"Hi, Maddie, Sophie, Nia, Amber, Sierra, McKenzie, Ava." My dad was pretty amazing with names and faces. He probably knew the first name of each and every person in school, as well as their dog. I still don't even know all of the names of everyone in seventh grade. Travis has over four hundred kids in seventh grade alone.

Dad walked over and put on a French accent. "How is *ze* food?"

The girls responded back to him in bad French accents, and then when he left everyone waved. *"Au Revoir."*

"Your dad's really cool, for a principal," said Nia.

"The best," chorused a few other girls.

Maddie glanced at me, as if to say, *See how nice Nia is?* I peered down at my chicken Frisbee sandwich on my tray, which would probably start another Nia lecture about the cruelty of eating animals with Maddie nodding along. She'd definitely been hypnotized by Nia. I looked longingly back at our regular table. I could see Heather and Nicole chatting together about something. I couldn't wait to go back to our old table tomorrow and tell them what it had been like sitting with Nia and the rest of the crew.

As the bell rang for fourth period, Nia turned to us and smiled. "See you later, goddess." This was Nia's new word of the week.

"See you, fellow goddess," said Maddie overenthusiastically. And a little geekily. I thought the word "fellow" sounded especially nerdy. Maddie had to watch it. Then when Nia was out of earshot, Maddie gushed, "She's so much nicer than I thought."

"Uh-huh," I said, although I was thinking, *I'm not so sure*. She set me up with the singing thing.

"I mean she looks a certain way. You know, with that hair and groovy clothes. But she went out of her way to include us and be nice."

"Uh-huh."

"Didn't you think she went out of her way?"

"She did do that," I admitted. "It's not like we've ever eaten with them before."

"I think Nia really likes us, Sophie. I'm thinking that seventh grade is going to be very interesting."

I didn't want seventh grade to be interesting. I wanted seventh grade to be just like sixth grade. I'd walk to Maddie's home, we'd have a snack, do some homework together. Chat when we got home while doing more homework. Spend Saturday night together, and my dad would get us Slurpees. We'd hang out with Heather and Nicole sometimes. That was all just fine with me. I wasn't so sure that I needed "interesting." But it looked like now that the Hot List was out, I didn't have much of a choice. I fantasized again about wiping it clean, but then I remembered it was permanent. I could sneak a can of paint to school, but that wasn't a good idea, especially for the principal's kid.

The next day at school, Nia invited us to eat with her again, which I thought was even weirder. I realized that Nia and Maddie had the art thing together, but I still didn't get why she'd wanted us—well, mostly Maddie—to eat at her table. I tried to protest and say what about Heather and Nicole, but Nia insisted that they were fine eating on their own. I considered going over to sit with them myself but that would be weird. I mean, it was Maddie who I really wanted to sit with anyway.

One more day of eating at Nia's table became two more days, and two more days became three more days. And suddenly, I found myself expecting to sit with Nia and the rest of the crew. On the second day, though, Heather and Nicole had approached me by my locker. "What's the deal with you and Maddie eating over with Nia and all of them? Can't sit with us since we're not on the Hot List?" She looked and sounded pretty hurt.

"Well, we're not on the List either. It was Maddie's idea. I'm missing sitting with you guys, though." And that was partly true. I didn't miss Heather and Nicole so much as sitting at the quiet end of a table alone with Maddie.

"Why don't you say something to Maddie?" asked Nicole.

"I'll try," I mumbled. Nicole frowned but didn't say anything more.

Meanwhile, Maddie seemed to be spending more time with Nia. She went over to her house to work on some videos. And then, using her calligraphy skills, she helped Nia decorate the Hot Listers' lockers with bolts of lightning and fire.

When I asked Maddie about it before lunch, like what was the deal with their sudden, close buddy-buddy friendship, she said, "Nia and I have stuff in common."

"Like?"

"Cool parents and art."

I clenched my teeth when Maddie said "parents," since

that sort of left me out. I have a parent. Not parents. I can't ever remember having parents with an *s* because I was so young when my mom died. "Whatever," I said to Maddie. "I still can't see you guys hanging."

Maddie gave me an intense eye lock. "Why don't you like Nia?"

"I didn't say that. It's just that she's going out of her way. And it seems weird."

"You've got to start trusting people," said Maddie. And I thought about that. Could she be right? Was I too paranoid?

Probably not. Two weeks ago, at a class field trip to the Denver art museum, I had been paired up to be Nia's buddy. As we walked through the exhibits, she had spent the entire time texting on her phone. Nia had gotten a chance to know me and was not interested. Then last Thursday when she had asked me if I wanted to go swimming after a soccer game, I had said no because I was pretty sure her mother had put her up to it.

I was about to explain it all to Maddie when Nia rushed up and dragged us to her table.

We talked about a TV show everyone was watching and how dumb the new school dress policy was about no more sandals. "Like toes are evil," said Nia. "It's healthy to air out your feet. I'm going to bring this up to student leadership."

As my dad strolled by she waved at him. "Mr. Fanuch."

"Fanuchi," I corrected.

Nia smiled. "I know, of course. But I like Fanuch. It sounds fun." She waved her arms with all of those colored hair bands and called out more loudly. "Mr. Fanuch, I have something to talk to you about."

My dad walked over to the table. "Yeeeees, I'm listening."

"It's the new dress policy," said Nia in her self-important voice. "No more open-toed shoes. It's prejudiced against sandals."

"And toes," reminded Ava.

"Exactly. They need to be aired out. Feet expand in the heat and closed shoes actually might cause damage, which could lead to lawsuits." Nia's eyes narrowed. She thought she was so clever.

"I see your point," said Dad, talking in a mock-presidential way. "But I can tell you that you wouldn't want to see some people's toes. They can be kind of scary. If you want to call a toe summit, it's fine with me."

"Thanks, Mr. Fanuch!" gushed Nia. After Dad was out of earshot, Nia said, "He's pretty awesome." Then I waited for her to add *And my mom thinks so too*. I still hadn't told Maddie that our parents were dating for a couple of weeks solid. So much time had passed, I feared telling her. I wasn't sure when it had moved from casual to seeing each other all of the time, but it had.

"Yeah, he's a pretty great dad," I admitted, relieved that Nia hadn't said anything about the dating situation. "Even if he's clueless about anything to do with technology. He doesn't know how to change the wallpaper on his phone."

"That's so sad," said Nia.

"Luckily, I save him," said Maddie, grinning. We high-fived each other, and, for a split second, I saw this look in Nia's eyes. Almost like she was a little jealous, which was weird because she was always surrounded by her groupies. I didn't get it. Why would she be jealous of us? "That's my job, saving people," continued Maddie.

"And you saved us from complete boredom this year by creating the Hot List."

Then Nia covered her mouth. "Whoops, I wasn't supposed to say that."

I stared at Maddie in complete disbelief. "What? You told? There is just no way." Whoa. I wasn't expecting this. Maddie's face grew pale, and Nia flicked an *I'm-sorry* look at her.

All of the chatter in the cafeteria suddenly went on high volume. The grease and meat loaf smells got smellier, and the lights brighter and blinkier. Everything was so awful I couldn't believe it. I felt like this couldn't be happening to me. This had to be happening to someone else. It was almost like I had stepped outside my own body, and I was watching my life in a horror movie.

And that's when I walked out of the caf.

I wanted to run, but I could feel eyes on me, so I slowed down just to look a little more relaxed and casual, yet purposeful. Like I had to leave to go a dentist appointment for a cleaning.

Of course, I had never been less relaxed or casual in my life. My cheeks felt hot, and I had to clench my fists tightly, so I wouldn't scream out loud. And I moved as calmly as you could in a cafeteria crowded with boys who stuck French fries up their noses, and blew up brown paper bags to pop like firecrackers, and a best friend who betrayed the biggest secret of your life.

Chapter Six

I walked out of the caf, outside in the courtyard, where there wasn't any Maddie. Or Nia. Or a Hot List.

My impulse was to leave school grounds. I just wanted to get as far away from Travis as I could.

I wanted to be alone in my room, where I could sniffle and listen to my iPod at full volume.

I couldn't cry in class, so the cafeteria courtyard would have to do. As I opened the door to go outside, a gust of wind hit my face. It was nippy, and I didn't have my coat, but I wasn't turning around. I kicked a nearby trash can like I was blocking a soccer ball from entering enemy territory.

And, to me, it felt like my own best friend was now the enemy.

Even though there were groups of kids standing around, nobody seemed to have noticed my kick. The courtyard was known as the place for students who didn't really do lunch—the skate rats who practiced tricks on imaginary skateboards, the girls with raccoon-mascara-type eyes, who carved their initials into picnic benches with their protractors, and the wannabe tough guys who did chicken fights. It was not the tattletale crowd.

Perfect, I thought. I was going to stay out here for the rest of lunch. Maddie could hang out inside with her new clan and her new way of speaking. "I'm so sad" and "evil." Ugh.

Maddie was, like, a jillion times evil for revealing our Hot List identities. A lifetime quota, as far as I was concerned.

I stared at the trash can that I had just kicked, which had been painted by student leadership last year in a campaign by Nia, of course. That little thought made me happy—I guess because I had kicked it.

Someone, probably Nia herself, had painted yellow sunflowers and written the message, DON'T HARM ANIMALS. What flowers and animals had to do with each other I had no idea.

There were other trash cans with other messages, like DON'T POLLUTE and DON'T LITTER, which seemed dumb to me. Because if you're the kind of person who's dumping your garbage in a trash can, you don't need to be reminded to not pollute.

Maddie needed a trash can that said DON'T BE A TRAITOR.

Suddenly, my throat felt achy. Why did Nia need Maddie? I couldn't figure it out. She had four other friends. Why did she need to add my best friend to her collection?

Ex-best friend, a little voice said in my head.

I didn't need her. In fact, I never wanted to see her again.

But my break from Maddie didn't last too long. A few seconds later, she raced into the courtyard. And not far behind her stood Nia. And then came McKenzie, Ava, Sierra, and Amber. They looked like little ducklings waddling behind their mother duck.

Great. Now the entire group of ducklings was watching me cry. Because that's what was happening. Actual tears were coming out of my eyes. I bent my head so nobody could see.

"I want to talk to you," called out Maddie, as she marched over to me.

I hugged my knees and stared at the ground. I watched a pill bug, scurrying over a large crack in the cement, only to fall in a few seconds later. His little legs were moving, as he turned upside down, but he wasn't going anywhere. He had fallen into the bug pit of doom.

I took my fingernail and scooped the little bug out of the crevice.

There was no way I was going to speak to her.

"Please," said Nia. "She can explain."

I could feel myself about to lose it. The tightness in my throat made it hard to swallow.

"I'm so sorry," said Maddie. "But don't blame Nia. It's so my fault."

I looked up. "That's right. It's *your* fault." I could feel some drops of rain coming down from the sky. And a breeze, which gave me goose bumps along my arms, so I hugged myself tighter. The other girls squealed as the raindrops began to fall. They all dashed back inside, except Maddie. She stood out in the rain. Her glasses got so fogged up I could hardly see her eyes.

"Say something," she said.

"Not with Nia here." I could see Nia peeking through an open door. Maddie looked pleadingly at Nia, who nodded and retreated back into the caf.

"Okay, I get why Nia was suddenly extra interested in being your friend. You told her that we created the Hot List."

"That's not why," insisted Maddie.

"How could you have embarrassed me like that? I mean, if you told Nia and all of them you might as well have broadcasted it on Denver TV for that matter. I'm sure *everyone* knows by now."

"That's not true. Nia isn't like that. Neither are the others. She knows we threw away the pen. That it was a one-time thing." She gave me a desperate look.

"Right. Like I'm going to have anything to do with the Hot List again. Seriously. How could you tell her? I thought I could trust you."

"Yeah, and I thought *you* trusted me." The rain came down harder so that even the skate rats, the raccoon-eyed girls, and the chicken-fighting boys rushed inside.

"What's that supposed to mean?"

"Never mind." Maddie stared at the cement.

"What? Tell me."

"Nia told me." She paused. "About your parents dating."

If it was possible, the chill outside felt chillier. I should have seen this coming I told myself. "I wanted to tell you," I began. "It's just been . . ."

"You know I've only really known Nia well for, what? Three weeks, and she's already telling me stuff that you can't. How do you think it makes me feel? It makes me wonder what else are you keeping from me? I told Nia because I trust her and she trusts me."

"So, are you and Nia best friends now?"

"I don't like that expression, 'best friend.' Nia says it's

hierarchal. I can have more than one friend, Sophie. I can be her friend, too."

"I don't think so," I said. Maddie had always been my best friend. She had known what it was like for me to grow up without a mom. There was no one else that could possibly understand.

"Are you making me choose?" asked Maddie. "That's not fair. I'm not going to do it."

"Fine," I said.

I felt like I could freeze-frame this moment. That from here on out everything would be different. What was mine was no longer mine. Maddie and Sophie were no longer Maddie and Sophie.

I was being spread around like I was a jar of peanut butter, all over the courtyard. Making the whole place sticky and deadly.

Yes, deadly, as I'm allergic to peanut butter—one taste and I break into hives and my breathing gets all wonky. I can't get my full breath until someone jabs me with my EpiPen. If not, I will die.

The peanut butter was spreading. Maddie was spreading it. . . .

And that was that. That was the day, the moment that our friendship ended, in the rain, after me eating half a chicken Frisbee sandwich.

The first thing I did when I got home was to throw away the scarf that Maddie had given me as a birthday present when she went to Barcelona again last summer. Her whole family goes every year because of her dad's work. I had been psyched to see Maddie when she had come back since she been away for weeks, and we had a lot to catch up on.

"Are you mad at me for not calling?" Maddie had asked.

"Of course not. I got the postcards and the e-mails," I said.

That's when she handed me the blue-green scarf. "I bought it on Las Ramblas, a marketplace street. Everyone was wearing them. Do you like it?"

It sparkled and was gauzy, almost like something Nia would wear, but I loved it.

"Smell it. It still smells like Barcelona. Olives, fried potatoes, and those sausage thingies they plop on toasted bread. All of it. It's just like mine, except mine is lavender. See?" She pulled hers out of a bag.

"It's great."

"I knew you would just LOVE it!"

I stood there and hugged her. "Soul sister power," I said.

"Soul sister power," she whispered back.

I remember she had signed all of her postcards like that. *Soul sisters, Maddie*. I went through my drawer and got them out. I intended to put them in the trash too. But I couldn't help reading them.

Sophie,
I'm in love with all of the cool museums and stuff in Barcelona and the human statues and the cute guy from England who I rode the boat with and who gave me his e-mail. But my mom threatened me that if I ever e-mailed him she would ground me for a thousand years and then she ripped up the paper that he wrote it on. Only I memorized part of the e-mail. It was eclipseson@something but I couldn't remember the second part of it. I tried AOL and some other ones but they didn't work, which is terrible because maybe we were meant to be, but because I can't remember a few letters we will be separated for eternity.
Soul sisters,
Maddie

And there was one that came four days later from Costa Brava, which is the gorgeous cliffy coast outside of Barcelona.

Sophie,

I think it's weird how at the beaches the girls wear
no tops, even like really old ladies who were all wrinkly
and I thought there was just no way I could ever do
something like that . . . and how my mom got her wallet
taken in the park when she put it down to buy lemonade
at a stand and how irritating it was that we didn't have
cell reception and my dad wouldn't stop at the Internet
café because we had "an itinerary." More castles today!
Soul sisters,
Maddie

After I read the postcards a couple of times, I tossed
them along with the scarf in the trash. I was going to throw
away the journal, too, but my dad walked into the room.

He peered at me curiously. "Is everything okay? At
school."

"Yes," I snapped. "Everything's just fine."

"You can express how you feel in a normal tone of voice."

"Okay," I said. "I'm using a normal tone of voice now.
And I'm telling you I just have a ton of homework. And
that's all."

When I went to school the next day, it was horrible,
especially since Maddie and I had our lockers so close

together. I couldn't look at her, and she wouldn't look at me. And during lunch, I could see Nia and the rest of the crew glancing at me and whispering.

I ate with Heather and Nicole, only it didn't go so well. As I went to sit down with them, they both glared at me. "Are we suddenly good enough to eat with now that you and Maddie had a fight?"

"You were always great to eat with," I said weakly.

"Didn't seem like it last week," said Nicole. "Or the week before, right?"

"Well, I didn't want to seem rude. Nia is pretty persuasive, and Maddie really wanted me to sit with her."

Nicole stabbed her broccoli spears. "But, basically, you have no place to sit because you and Maddie aren't talking anymore. And we're convenient."

"No, that's not it. I've always liked you guys."

I could see that this wasn't working, so I picked up my tray to go.

"Stop." Nicole put her hand up. "You can eat with us." So, like a pathetic loser, I stayed because I didn't know where else to go. I couldn't have eaten with girls from my soccer team because I play club and they're mostly at different schools. And the girls who do go to my school are in eighth grade and have a different lunch period.

So I ended up eating with Heather and Nicole, but it

was awful sitting there without Maddie and enduring their stony silence. I felt like a third wheel. I kept waiting for Maddie to come over to be me, but she didn't. Everywhere I went it was hard to avoid her because we have so many classes together. And each day was pretty much torture because I felt like I didn't have anyone to talk with other than just acquaintances. Maddie, of course, continued to sit on the other side of the cafeteria with Nia and her clan. If I were a cave girl I could drag her back to my table. But I wasn't a cave girl. I was Sophie, a regular seventh grader, without a best friend.

Chapter Seven

After the slowest month of my life, another Hot List came out on the first Monday in October. It was so weird because our Hot List had come out the first Monday in September. And somehow, it was once again written up with the same sparkly pen and all caps. I figured someone must have definitely recovered the pen out of the garbage when I buried it into the trash. Who it was, I wasn't sure, but I thought it could be someone from the drama club since they had been practicing those one-acts. Although it might not even be one person. There was a rumor that it was a group who called themselves the Sisterhood of the Traveling Pen and that each month someone different in the group would be responsible for creating the List.

But it was just a rumor.

Anyway, the whole school went crazy talking about the

new Hot List. The names were almost the same but there were some changes. The biggest one was that Maddie was now on the Hot List, number fourteen.

It was probably because Maddie was now wearing contacts, cut out the lavender look, and was wearing layered, flowing tunics with stacked necklaces and lots of bangles, like another clone in the hippie-chic clan. Auggie moved down to third place and Hayden stayed on first. And a couple of guys were knocked off. The same stuff happened with everyone making a big deal out of the whole thing. They thought—especially Nia—that the whole thing was mystical practically. Like the List created cuteness in people, which was so weird.

I figured that Maddie and Nia and the rest of them had written up the new Hot List. It made me so mad that, when I saw Maddie by her locker during the break between first and second period, I had to say something.

"So you did the Hot List without me?" I said to Maddie. "And put yourself on it."

Maddie tried to shut her locker, but a few notebooks were sticking out, so she couldn't. "Oh, you're talking to me now?"

"Obviously."

She tried to slam her locker, but I didn't budge. I didn't go to stack her books neatly on her shelf. Maddie eyed me, stood on tiptoe and did it herself. "I don't know who did the List, which is kind of cool. Magic, even." She shrugged, and I thought that "magic" comment sounded like Nia. "Nobody knows who's doing it."

"C'mon. You and Nia must have done it."

Maddie held up her hand. "I swear. You don't have to believe me. But it's not my handwriting anyway."

And she was right. It had definitely been the same ink, but it wasn't her handwriting. She couldn't help but make things a little too perfect-looking.

"Anyway," said Maddie. "It's kind of cool. Isn't it?"

No, it really wasn't cool. Nothing to do with the Hot List was cool. At least to me. Not anymore. Not when Maddie was becoming a whole other person I hardly recognized. She had started to curl her hair, so she could capture a little of the flowing rock-star-locks look. Her hair was still short, but I could tell that she was growing it.

I regretted the day I ever started the Hot List. Really I did it all to impress Maddie, but that definitely didn't work. I thought about that morning when it had all began and wished I could take it all back. That moment when I created the concept of the Hot List in the first place.

And it wasn't just me who felt that way. Between second and third period I passed Brianna Evans, the flirt

76

and gossip from homeroom. She was blowing her nose. "What's wrong?" I asked.

"Nothing," she said.

Her eyes were red and she stared absently into space.

Then she blinked like she was missing her contacts and she couldn't see.

"What's wrong?" I repeated. I could tell that something was really bothering her.

"Oh, it's just that Bear wasn't being his usual flirty self today in homeroom."

"Okay, maybe he was tired. Or overslept."

"No, that's not it."

"So, he was, like, being a jerk to you?"

"Yeah."

"C'mon. Tell me."

"It's because I'm not on the Hot List, and he got on. He stared all morning at Amber."

She sniffed and the tip of her nose was as red as Rudolph's.

"Okay. Sounds like it's not a real problem. It'll blow over. It's just the freshness of it all."

She shook her head. "And what . . . if I'm not ever on the Hot List." She shrugged. "What can I do? There's nothing to do."

Brianna's incessant flirty peppiness with Bear sort of

made me sick, but they were always so pully, grabby, and happy. It really made me feel bummed to see her all sad. It was against the laws of nature or something.

During lunch, I told Heather and Nicole all about Brianna. And for the first time eating with them didn't suck. Heather was a good listener and Nicole made me laugh with her comments about Brianna. Now that she was unable to flirt with Bear, we'd be spared watching them tie each other's shoelaces together all of the time and doing that mock-growling thing. So just as I was feeling almost happy, on the way to fourth period, I spotted Maddie and Nia arm-in-arm skipping down the hall. I couldn't help listening in on their conversation.

"Maybe we can decorate Hayden and Auggie's lockers after the leadership meeting. No one will be around," said Nia.

"Absolutely," agreed Maddie.

"I'm thinking lightning bolts. On fashiontween.com they're all about lightning."

"Count me in!" said Maddie.

"Today is a good day. I feel good!"

"I feel good too!" said Maddie.

"I feel gooder!" Nia said even louder.

"I feel gooder bestest," said Maddie, laughing.

And there was no doubt about it, I felt the worst.

After school, I threw myself on my bed and listened to mostly depressing songs on my iPod. I didn't do any homework, I didn't get dinner started. I just stared at the ceiling with a sad soundtrack going.

Of course, when my dad came home, he noticed me acting like a slug. Without knocking he barged into my room, sat on the edge of my bed, and said he wanted to talk to me about something. "Are you upset with me dating Mrs. Tate?" He seemed so happy that I didn't feel like saying anything, so I shook my head. Of course, I didn't love the idea of my dad dating, but I did understand. They had been seeing each for a solid month now, and Mrs. Tate couldn't help that she was Nia's mom.

Then Dad cleared his throat and started asking me why Maddie wasn't coming around anymore, and I broke down and told him that we had a fight. I didn't give him any more details than that. "I'm sorry, honey," he said. "I really am. But that happens to friends sometimes. Even"— he cupped his mouth confidentially—"to administrators. There are a couple of curriculum developers in the superintendent's office who are not on speaking terms right now. Even your mom and I used to fight."

I smiled a little. Dad hadn't spoken about Mom in awhile. I liked it when he did because it brought her back a little. I had been in preschool when she had died, so my memories of her mostly come from our family albums and videos.

"Mom and I fought about dumb stuff," said Dad, as he picked up my soccer ball and twirled it in his hand. "The laundry. Who was supposed to pay a bill."

"Well, it's not dumb stuff between me and Maddie. I can't trust her anymore."

"You guys have been friends for so long. Can I call her parents? Maybe we could bring you guys together to work this out?"

"No, don't you dare do that, Dad! No. Please."

"It might be good for me to check in with Maddie's parents. We could help. I do have a counseling degree."

"Don't do it! You can't!"

"Okay, okay. I just hate seeing you so miserable."

Get used to it, I thought.

Chapter Eight

Texts received on Nia Tate's Phone: 14

      Homeroom

      Travis Middle School

      Boulder, Colorado

      USA

      Monday, November 2

      Between 8:27 a.m. and 8:31 a.m.

      Central Time

Texts received on Maddie Narita's Phone: 6

      Homeroom

      Travis Middle School

      Boulder, Colorado

      USA

      Monday, November 2

      Between 8:27 a.m. and 8:31 a.m.

      Central Time

Texts received on Sophie Fanuchi's Phone: 0

      Homeroom

      Travis Middle School

      Boulder, Colorado

      USA

      Monday, November 2

      Between 8:27 a.m. and 8:31 a.m.

      Central Time

It was the first Monday in November, and the rumor was that another Hot List would be posted today. Everyone was chatting and gossiping about it. While the old Hot Lists eventually got painted over, the others were texted, tweeted, e-mailed, and video-blogged. It was the start of second period, and everyone was waiting for a Hot List sighting.

I watched Nia glance down at her phone, which she strategically hid in her desk.

"I wonder if anyone new is going to get on," Nia said to Maddie, who unfortunately sat in front of me in pre-algebra. Mrs. Tate had a seating chart, so I couldn't move to the back of the classroom like I wanted.

Mrs. Tate—my teacher, and Nia's mom, and my dad's pretty-much girlfriend after two months of regular dating—was giving us ten minutes of individual review time before the quiz, so some kids were still hauling their math books out of their backpacks, while others flipped through their binders. Some girls glanced down at their hidden phones. Mrs. Tate has the same moon-shaped face and curly blond hair as Nia, except hers was shorter.

Mrs. Tate approached Maddie's desk and set her lips into a line. "I have to take your phone. Hand it over." Mrs. Tate's Southern drawl made the command seem nicer somehow.

"Sorry," said Maddie, giving Mrs. Tate her cell, who imprisoned it in a drawer in her desk. And then she wrote Maddie's name up on the whiteboard. "You can pick it up after school."

Pre–Hot List, pre-Nia, Maddie would have never gotten her name written up on the board.

"And you too, Nia," Mrs. Tate said.

Nia sighed and handed over her phone, and Mrs. Tate wrote her up. I had to like Mrs. Tate for a moment. When it came to enforcing the rules, she didn't skip over her daughter.

I stared outside the window, where I could catch a peek of the blue outline of the Rocky Mountains. Usually, looking at the snow-capped peaks made me happy but not today. List Day reminded me of what happened between Maddie and me.

I watched as Nia dug out her binder and slammed it onto her desk. I knew she was mad at her mom.

The other kids were all whispering about the Hot List as they wrote down the assignment, which was in the right corner of the whiteboard, while Mrs. Tate watered her fica. It kept dropping crunchy, yellow leaves.

The quiet chatting continued, and Mrs. Tate said, "I suggest all eyes stay focused on the quiz." She handed out the stacks of quizzes to the first desk on every row to pass back. "Do what I say, and y'all will do real well on your big test coming up," she continued, as if we were sixth graders and not seventh graders, practically high school students.

Actually, if you wanted to do well at Travis, there was *only* one thing you really needed to pay attention to today, and it was the List. Unfortunately.

"You've got to go to the bathroom for me!" yelled Squid, during the break between second and third period. He stood behind me, pleading.

"Excuse me?" I whipped around in the hall to face Squid, who wore a green gymnastics T-shirt and purple athletic shorts. "You want *me* to go to the bathroom for *you*?" I stared at his crazy mullet haircut. And the row of pimples dotting his forehead. "Are you sick or something?" Other students poured around us, trying to get to their lockers before fourth period. A line of girls darted out of the bathroom. Some shook their heads, while others had huge smiles on their faces.

Squid raised his eyebrows like I was the one who was crazy. "Sophie, I mean go *into* the bathroom." I stared at a ray of afternoon sun poking through one of the few windows in the hallway. "Why would you want me to go into the bathroom for you?"

"I want you to see whether I'm on it."

"On what?" I shrugged and glanced at the hall clock.

"You know what I'm talking about." Of course I knew. Like the first time, the Hot List was once again being posted in the girls' bathroom. But I wasn't going to let on that I knew it. A couple of seventh-grade girls strolled by and pretended to be interested in the talent show poster. But really they were glancing at me as Squid pointed and twirled his finger like I was insane. The girls snickered nervously. Even though I didn't want to care, I did.

In the hall Squid continued to beg. In fact, he was hopping on one foot, as if that would impress me. I think it just made him look like he needed to go the bathroom. Doors to the cafeteria swung open and a bunch of guys with oversize backpacks moved past us.

"Please, Sophie," he pleaded. "Go into the bathroom and look. See if I'm on the List." Just because I no longer had any real friends, he assumed we were best buddies.

"I want to get to my locker, Squid, so move it." It was almost the end of lunch period so I had about ten minutes to dump my books off at my locker and cram for the vocab quiz in English. I stared at Squid's T-shirt. Was that tomato sauce ringing his collar? Probably because he shoveled in the ravioli they were serving during lunch. "What are you talking about anyway?"

He darted a glance at a trio of girls strolling past and whispered so nobody could hear, "The Hot List."

"Oh, that." I sighed.

"Just the thing that defines everyone's status at this school," said Squid. The crazy thing was that even though I had invented the List, even though it had been around for just a couple of months, it felt like the List had always been there.

According to Nia and her crew, the List determined everything. If you weren't on the Hot List, you just weren't hot. Getting on the Hot List equaled social success and happiness.

The Hot List Facts

Fact: When Micah Wong got on the Hot List he got voted most valuable player on the soccer team. And everyone knew that Micah was a just a so-so player who mostly ran around in circles while his teammates did most of the hard work.

Fact: When Anson Blovack went from number eleven to number five on the Hot List, he started juggling three different girlfriends in two different schools for more than two months. And everyone knew before that Anson had only one girlfriend. For two days . . . and twenty-two seconds.

Fact: When Teddy Stella got elevated to number two, he got 167 new friends on Facebook in one day. And two girls left messages in his in-box that they were willing to fold his laundry.

And today, sometime during fourth period, on November 2, a new Hot List had definitely been posted. New names went on and, of course, some got the big boot.

I was planning on NOT checking it out as a personal protest to all the List hysteria, even though I was definitely curious.

I stared at Squid, who was still hopping. But this time there were no onlookers. Apparently there were some people at this school still eating their lunch. "You're *not* serious," I said, "about going into the bathroom to see the List. Tell me you're not."

He pressed his hands together in a praying position.

"Okay, you're serious."

He nodded so the tail part of his mullet-style hair flipped up in the back. As a media center assistant pushing a cart with A/V equipment clattered down the hallway, I waved my hand in Squid's face. "The whole thing's *so* lame. And I have to get ready for Casey's class or I'll be toast." I took a step down the hallway, away from the bathroom.

"WAIT! Don't go!" He grabbed my sweater. "I just have to find out. That's all. I heard from someone who heard it from someone that I might be on it."

"Geez, you don't give up. Why should I go into the bathroom for you? You know I don't care about stuff like the List."

"It's *because* you don't care. I couldn't ask"—he pointed to a band of girls clicking away down the hall in their cookie-cutter outfits from the mall—"them. But you're different. You're all . . ."

"What . . . I'm all what?" I put my hand on my hip and considered drop-kicking him. I could, given the fact that I'm probably six inches taller than him. Me, Sophie, tall girl. And then there was Squid, short boy. I guess it made us the middle school equivalent of a Great Dane and a toy poodle.

Squid gazed up at me. "You're, like, above it all or something." Yeah, I was above *him*. Like, at least by half a foot, even if my new boots did have a little heel on them today.

I smiled and patted his head again. "Thank you, Squid. That's the first decent thing you've said all day."

"You're welcome," he gushed, gazing up at me with a goofy smile. That's when I turned around to see a girl swatting her friend with a cell phone and a bunch of sixth-grade guys stopping up the water fountain with paper towels to create a flood.

"I'm *so* done with middle school." For many good reasons. At least winter break was next month.

Squid threw out his arms. "I'm not done with middle school. I want to be on the List at least before Christmas." He smiled so his dimples popped out and showed his crooked teeth, which were railroaded with red braces.

"Will you PLEASE go in there?" he pleaded, getting down on one knee.

Being in Drama Club for the past year and a half really left its ridiculous imprint on him. I craned to see the clock in the hallway. "Gotta go, Squid. I have, like, three minutes to dump my books in my locker before—"

He snatched my social studies textbook. "I'll carry them for you!"

"I don't need your help, Squid." Then a bunch of kids came barreling out of the cafeteria, including Hayden. Blue. Live and inperson. As he strutted down the hall my heart stuttered. Hayden was so cute he could easily be a celebrity. He turned toward me and saluted, mumbling, "Hey," and I was about to utter back *Hey* all coolly when Squid screamed, "SOPHIE, NUMBER ONE JUST SAID HI TO YOU!"

By number one, of course, he meant number one on the Hot List. Hayden probably thought this also meant that he was my number one.

Which he was, of course. I could feel the heat in my cheeks like it was mid-July.

Hayden was now walking backward and grinning as he twirled his lacrosse stick. "And now I'm saying bye. Bye, Sophie!"

Would the linoleum just open up and swallow me now? I weakly nodded bye to him. How could Squid do this to me? Hayden turned around and was now casually strolling away with one hand in his jean pocket, and the other holding his lacrosse stick.

That was so Hayden.

Also, he never wore a dorky backpack like other guys. I

wasn't sure how he transported regular things like books, erasers, and his lunch. Maybe someone did that for him.

If he asked, I would even do it.

I had this feeling that by high school, he would be discovered by a Hollywood casting agent. Slowly, we would start hanging out and become a couple based on mutual admiration. The Hollywood establishment would be baffled as to why the famous actor did not go for a model, but he preferred to stay home with me, by the fire in our Swiss-style chalet in Boulder.

Of course, he'd take me to all of the Hollywood A-list parties. We'd have four children—two girls and two boys—he would offer me four nannies to care for them but I would say no, what with their dimples and . . .

Squid pushed against my shoulder. "Say bye back to him!"

At this point, Hayden was a dot down the other side of the hall.

"No, shut up, Squid," I said, groaning under my breath and pulling my hoodie further around my face. "There's no way!"

"Afraid Hayden Carus'll know you like him?" He raised his eyebrows knowingly.

Ah, no. That ship had already sailed, probably.

As Squid jumped to his feet, I noticed how he had

bleached his sneakers with these weird eyeball patterns. Suddenly, I had to get away from him. And the bathroom was my quickest escape. And, okay, my curiosity about the List had won out.

"See you later, Squid. I'm going in but don't expect me to report back to you. You'll just have to ask someone else." That was when I pushed back Squid like I was a firefighter about to save a Chihuahua from a burning building.

Chapter Nine

I rammed the bathroom door open with my shoulder and spotted Maddie at the sink, applying some gooey moisturizing lotion that smelled like over-ripe mangoes. And Nia was next to her, applying the exact same kind. Matching crystals hung at their necks. They both stood there, in peasant shirts and stacked necklaces and suede boots, chatting away.

"I can't believe he stayed on the List," said Nia, shaking her head. "I mean, zits." She tapped her nose.

"I know. Seriously," agreed Maddie. "What were they thinking?"

As I stood there in front of the door, Nia shook back her corkscrew blond curls. "I still think you should ask Auggie to the skate park. For a little private lesson."

"You think?" asked Maddie, reddening a little.

I couldn't believe it. Maddie and Nia were actually talking about the List as if they didn't write it. I guess I was wrong to think they were the new listmakers. That left me with tons of unanswered questions. Like who actually was the Listmaker? Was Maddie still on? Was Hayden still number one? Could I be on? Nah, that wasn't happening.

I strode purposefully into the bathroom and stopped by the last stall, the new and original home of the List, and waited behind a strawberry blond-headed girl with pigtails.

"And did you see Vinday got onto the List?" went Nia. Then she saw me and suddenly stopped speaking. I expected them to run away from me like I was the "it" in a game of hide-and-seek.

"Hey," I said, trying hard to give them my *I-don't-care* face. Seeing them together made my stomach muscles bunch up.

They both gave me grade-A fake smiles. They were so obsessed with the Hot List. They probably wouldn't leave the bathroom for the rest of the day. Just so they could be near the List. And moisturize with organic products. You'd think they lived in the Mojave Desert and not outside of Denver.

Nia turned away as Maddie shrugged and gave me a guilty look.

I noticed her hair had grown out and was now almost

touching her shoulders and had a lot more body. She must have gotten some kind of a perm of something. I couldn't help but check myself out in the mirror. Yeah. The same brown eyes and long dark brown, almost black, hair that touched my shoulders. But it wasn't flowy like Nia's or Maddie's. It was straight as a board.

Sighing, I headed into the stall and checked out the lame-o list.

There was still Hayden Carus at the top. I started by reading from the top of the guys' list:

HAYDEN CARUS
TEDDY STELLA
AUGGIE MARTIN
TYLER FINKEL
ANSON BLOVACK
MATT JAMES
NICK HYDE
ARI SILVERS
TYSON BLANDERS
GEORGE MCGOWAN
FRANK PARSONS
KIRK DAVIES
SEAN MCCARTHY
RANDALL TANNER

JONAH BARKER
KEIFER PHILLIPS
BEAR ARVANITES
VINDAY PATEL
SERGIO RALETA
MICAH WONG

And next to it was the girls' list.

NIA TATE
AVA ALLEN
SIERRA BLACKSTONE
MCKENZIE DARLINGTON
AMBER SMITH
ADIA STILLER
MEI WONG
ALYSON HERNANDEZ
MADDIE NARITA
LISA GREGORY
SIERRA STEVENS
LESLIE GOTTFRIED
SARAH RUINSKY
JANE COCKRELL
LIESA SALEEM
CLARA PESSEREAU

SHERRY WARE
RUBY KUMAR
JENNY GOLD
LEAH PFEIFFER

The List was so long that it ran to the bottom of the door. Of course, Squid's name wasn't there. But when I glanced at the girls' list there were a couple of surprises. I still wasn't on the Hot List, but Maddie had pulled up to number nine, even ahead of Sierra. Nia, of course, was still number one followed by Ava. Some things never changed, except friendships. I think Maddie's sister, Gwen, had been right about seventh grade after all.

Chapter Ten

As I got out of the stall, I could hear Nia and Maddie speaking as they applied lip gloss by the sink. When they saw me walk out, Nia said, "Sorry you didn't get on."

"I don't care," I snapped.

"Are you mad at me because you don't have the power of the List anymore?"

"No," I whispered back.

"Because it's beyond you. There's this energy around the List." She clutched her crystal necklace. "It's big. It's bigger than any of us."

"People make the List, not energy from your crystal." Then I lowered my voice even more. "I might not have the pen anymore, but I know how to get someone on the List. Look at Maddie. She started hanging with you, dresses the part, and then, voila, she's on. It'd be true for anyone."

"No, it's so beyond that," said Nia in her New Agey way.

"Exactly," agreed Maddie.

Nia stood back and pressed her lips together. "The List's like a perfect snapshot of hotness. It's eerie."

"It's freaky," said Maddie.

I had to speak up again. "It's because you guys both got on that you think it's all eerie and magical."

"That's so evil," said Nia. "It has nothing to do with that."

I stared at Maddie. "It's simple. Like I said, you got contacts and started wearing Nia's clothes. That's why you're on the Hot List."

Nia glared at me. "You enjoy being mad, don't you? It's so sad. You just can't handle us being friends."

I swallowed and then said, "What I can't handle is the way you go around acting like the Hot List 'knows.' People write the Hot List. Okay? It's people." I peered at Maddie meaningfully. "Hello. It doesn't just appear."

"Actually, I think it does," snapped Nia. "Nobody ever sees anyone writing it up. Ev-er. I'm not doing it. And neither is"—she ticked off names on her fingers—"Maddie, Ava, McKenzie, Amber, or Sierra."

"You think the Hot List has powers or something? It doesn't. Trust me. Maddie is on the List now because she changed her look. That's it. If I gave advice to the biggest loser at the school, I could get him up on the next List. No problem. It's people who start acting like models who get on the List. The List doesn't, like, give them a makeover. They do it to themselves."

Nia grabbed my hand. "We've got to talk," she said.

"Aren't we, like, talking right now?"

She shook her head so her corkscrew curls bounced. "I've got an idea. But it's kind of private. And involves both of us." She pointed to the stall, the one on the very end. "In there."

Only Nia would want to talk in a bathroom stall. She looked around at the other girls who began to stare at us. She shrugged. "Like I said, it's private."

"What about me?" asked Maddie.

"Sorry, just room for two," said Nia.

Maddie's frown made me feel a little bit happy. *She should know what it feels like to be left out,* I thought. I put on my *whatever* face and bravely headed for the stall. But what was I thinking? What did the person on my most-annoying list have to say to me now? My back pressed up against the giant toilet-paper dispenser. "So what's up, Nia?" I asked, pretending that I loved being stuck in a small space that smelled like bleach and bubble gum.

"You said you could get the biggest loser on the List."

"Uh-huh."

"So do it. 'Cause I don't think you can."

"What?"

"Afraid? That you're wrong." She looked at me knowingly.

"I could do it."

"If you can do it, then I'd do something completely psycho. Like"—she shut her eyes for a moment—"put on a fuzzy pink boa, tiara, and sparkly shoes, and in the middle of the caf, I'd give my crush the five things I like about him written on little heart-shaped pieces of paper."

Wow. That was insane. Did I really care that much about Nia to take this on? The better part of me knew I shouldn't, but a bigger part of me wanted to prove something. Like to Maddie how absurd the Hot List had become. And the fact that Nia could potentially, absolutely humiliate herself seemed like a worthwhile bonus.

"Cool," I said. "I'd so love to see you do that."

"But if you lose, *you'd* have to put on the tiara, pink fuzzy boa, and sparkly shoes. And"—she grinned happily—"in the middle of the caf do the five-things-I-like-about-you thing to your crush."

"Is this, like, a bet?"

"Exactly."

Ugh. That was as scary as the piece of paper that wouldn't flush in the List stall and was swirling around the toilet.

"Okay," I said. Because I was crazy at that exact moment. But mostly because Nia always made me feel like I was a loser. And I was *so* tired of it. When it came to Maddie, she had won the friendship battle. But I wasn't some wimpy pushover.

Right now I was going to get a chance to show them what I could do.

I smiled and tried not to breathe in bleach and bubble gum smell. "Yeah, I'll do it."

"Great." Nia fingered her colored beads. "You've got, like, a month to get some loser on the next Hot List."

"Not a problem. But there's one thing. How do I know that you're not the one writing the List or one of your friends? I mean, you could just leave off whoever I pick."

"I'm so not doing the List," she said, holding up her hand. "I swear on my grandfather." She blinked a few times. "He died last year, and, um, well, I wouldn't swear on him, if it wasn't true."

As much as I didn't like her fake-hippie, New-Agey-best-friend-stealing self, for some reason, I believed her. "We're on," I said and shook her hand. Her fingers were slimy from that mango moisturizer. "Now we just need to find this so-called loser."

Nia smiled at me like she was actually genuinely happy, whereas usually she acted like I was a rock in her knee-high boots. "You said anyone," she pointed out.

"Uh-huh."

"So *I* get to choose."

"Sure," I said, trying to outdo her with confidence. "Bring on the loser."

Chapter Eleven

A high-pitched squeal pierced through the bathroom.

"Boy!" screamed someone.

"Where?" Nia burst out of the stall, and, like a maniac, I rushed after her.

There stood Squid—SQUID RODRIGUEZ—staring at the List. He waggled his hips like he was auditioning for *Dancing With the Stars*. "Am I on it? I am, right? Right?" His eyes grew saucer round, and his tongue lolled out of his mouth. He looked like a giant puppy hungry for a treat.

"You've got to leave," said Nia. "Now!"

"You can't be here," said Maddie.

"Sorry," said Squid. "But I'm going in there." He pointed to the Hot List stall. A bunch of girls giggled.

"Go to the boy's bathroom, dude," stated Nia in her very bossy leadership-council voice. She pointed toward the door. "It's down the hall."

The girls inside the List stall burst out and backed away.

"I didn't mean you. I mean him." She pointed at Squid. "I said leave. You're a boy. This is a girls' bathroom. You can find out if you're on the List. But not in here."

Squid cut the line and marched right up to the List stall door. I couldn't believe he barged in like that. He was more of a geek/weirdo than I thought.

Everybody in the bathroom held their breath, which in the bathroom was probably always a good idea.

That was when Nia and Maddie rushed in front of him. Squid tried to push his way past but they were stronger.

And bigger. Not that it was saying much.

So Squid ducked right under them and into the stall.

Being small had its advantages.

Once inside, he went, "Aha" and "Oh" and "Interesting."

Maddie raced to my side. "What were you guys talking about? What did Nia want?"

I gave her a look: *Like I would tell you.* "Ask Nia."

"Fine," Maddie said, doing her frowny thing.

There were squeals as Squid exited the stall. Nia tried to grab him, but he slid out of her grasp.

"Get out!" she yelled. For a moment, I semi-liked Nia.

She was so determined to be rid of Squid, and that was a positive thing.

Squid guarded his turf, so Nia pushed against him like he was a volleyball, and then he lunged forward and walked on his hands. With his skills, I could definitely see him joining the circus, especially the clown show. A bunch of girls screamed and yelled, "Freak!"

That's when Mrs. Heidegger, the hall monitor, barreled into the bathroom. I quickly hunched over and pulled my hoodie down. Mrs. Heidegger raised her silver whistle to her mouth and inhaled a deep breath.

TWEEEEEEEEEEEEET!

I had to clap my hands over my ears because it was so ridiculously high and loud.

"Okay, clear out!" Mrs. Heidegger didn't need to ask me twice. I slinked out as the custodian spotted Squid. "What are you doing in here, buddy?"

Squid shrugged. "I had an emergency."

"Him," Nia said as we moved down the hallway.

"Him what?" I asked.

She nodded and smugly folded her arms in front of her chest.

"He's the one," she mouthed.

Then suddenly, I got it. Squid. I had to get Squid Rodriquez on the Hot List in one month. Sure, I had been decent at doing some wardrobe consulting with Maddie when we were friends. But this was waaaaaay different. I wasn't a miracle worker. I wasn't some twenty-first-century saint or something.

What on earth had I gotten myself into?

Chapter Twelve

The Top Five Reasons Why Speaking to Squid Is Impossible

1. He's weird and his weirdness might rub off on me like some kind of contagious disease.
2. He doesn't talk—he screams. And he will probably let everyone know, while screaming, that I have helped him do something lame.
3. He is not a television set so I can't turn down his volume.
4. He looks like a Lego figure—short, blocky, and cartoony. Only with Legos, you can take them apart and rebuild them into something better.
5. He smells like sweat socks and beef jerky.

Clumps of kids squeezed through the halls on their way to fifth period. So there I was, surrounded by other students, but still, I felt completely alone. This was because I knew I had to speak to Squid about getting him onto the Hot List. Part of me thought that this was ridiculous. I could avoid all of this by just sneaking into the bathroom and writing Squid's name up on the next Hot List.

But there were too many problems with that plan. I could get caught. And I didn't have the sparkly pen. Sure, I could buy something online, probably. But then, there was Squid. Unless he was actually hot, everyone would think my addition was a complete hoax.

I headed over to the south wing hallway where Squid and his friends usually hung out. We had a ten-minute break after fourth period, so a lot of people stuck by their lockers.

I easily spotted Squid because he was trying to walk up the front of his locker, just like those guys on YouTube. He charged forward, blasted halfway up, and then jumped down onto the floor, almost knocking down a couple of girls like they were bowling pins. I recognized them from being in the talent show last year.

They screamed, and he looked at them, wide-eyed.

"What do you think you're doing?" said the taller girl with a cool pixie haircut.

The smaller girl readjusted her glasses, which had slipped down her ski-jump nose. "Dude, get a grip," she said. "You don't have superpowers."

Squid grinned at them and pointed to his locker. "Oh, yeah, I do!" He rolled up his sleeves.

I could handle this. I cleared my throat and tried to act calm. "Um, Squid. I need to talk to you."

"About the bathroom incident?" He pulled a detention slip out of his pocket. "Nice, huh? Your dad personally gave it to me."

"Squid, I—"

He raised his hand. "Hold up and prepare to be a-mazed."

Instinctively, I stepped backward, as I had seen Squid do this maneuver once before on the aspen tree by the soccer field. Actually, he tried it, like, eleven times, and then on the eleventh, he fell on his back. It looked *really* painful.

He zoomed toward his locker, but then suddenly stopped. "Sorry, it's my dumb backpack." Squid glared at his orange backpack with its crazy assortment of stickers. Then he tossed if off, and it thwacked onto the ground. The two girls—I didn't know them that well—looked at each other, rolling their eyes as he tried it again, this time backing up farther so he could get a running start.

Squid sprinted faster and walked up even higher, landing harder on his rear. When he gazed at the muddy footprints, he gave a thumbs-up. It had been snowing a few days ago, but then it thawed, creating puddles of mud. And now that mud was on Squid's locker.

The girls tittered and strolled away.

Elio McMan, a chunky boy with a bowl haircut and wearing a *Star Trek* T-shirt, stared in admiration. "I think you're twenty inches from the top," he lisped.

"Maybe, possibly," said Gabriel Chowdry, a tall skinny guy with curly brown hair that stuck out like it had been shocked. He used his arm to measure the length of the muddy footprints. "But you can't be sure, since we don't have a measuring tape."

Squid sat up, bounced over to the locker and patted his hands onto the mud-spattered locker. "Twelve and a half inches, dude."

"Hey, Squid," I said. "I seriously have to talk to you." But he didn't hear me because he and his buddies were too busy arguing about how high up the footprints went on the locker.

"You don't know," persisted Gabriel. "Not unless you measure it."

"I can tell," said Squid, putting his hand over his heart. "My hand is exactly eight inches tall."

"My yo-yo string's exactly twenty-two inches. I could measure it with that." Elio cupped the yo-yo, then released it and put the string against the door. "Uh-huh. Twenty and a half exactly."

"Squid!" I practically shouted. This was not what I wanted. I did *not* want a scene. This was bad. "Squid!"

"You like my footprints? Want me to walk up your locker, Sophie?" This was SOOOOOOOOOOOOO wrong. What was I thinking?

"That's okay," I said, trying not to scream. I was smiling, in fact. Squid shouldn't see that I was annoyed. I was happy about this, really.

"Can we talk?" I said, keeping my voice even.

"Sorry." Squid waved his hands in front of his face. "Whatever else I did to you. Sorry."

"You don't have to apologize. I wanted to talk to you. About something. In private."

"Private! She wants to talk in private!" yelled Elio, who was spinning his yo-yo around with his fingers so that it practically jumped off the string. "Ewwwww."

"The digs chick me," said Squid, grinning. Then Elio and Gabriel started slapping their thighs and shrieking just like two monkeys I saw in the Denver Zoo. Only those monkeys were way cuter.

Squid edged toward me. "What do you want to talk

about, huh? Huh?" He opened his lips so I could see the red braces railroading his teeth.

"I'd like to help you, Squid. I'd like to help you get on the Hot List." *Ugh, did I really say that?*

"Help me get onto the Hot List? Okay, now I know I'm really being punked." He backed into his locker and mud from his footprints caked into his hair. "You didn't want to help me less than an hour ago. So I want to know why. Be honest."

"Why? Now, that's a great question." *Why? Because of Nia, that's why. Think happy thoughts.* I smiled like Peter Pan (who I used to have a crush on when I was six) was about to carry me off to Neverland, which would be a much better option than being here with Squid.

"Why do I want to help you? Because I want to prove something to someone who's extremely lame," I said, which was the true part. "And you've got natural potential. The most of any guy in the school." That was probably the hugest lie I'd ever told.

Elio and Gabriel were edging toward us. "Tell them to go away," I urged. "This is strictly a private conversation."

"But they're my bros."

"Squid," I warned.

"Shoo," he said. "Dudes, go away." They, unbelievably, did take a few steps back.

"I still don't get it," said Squid. "You think I'm a freak." He bugged out his eyes and pulled them down so I could see the whites. "Which I am."

And he was happy about that fact, which I *so* did not get.

I smiled harder. "I like to pretend to be annoyed with you, but I'm so sure, with a little help, you'd get on the List. I seriously love doing makeovers and stuff." Okay, that was an exaggeration. Back in fifth grade, Maddie and I did like to pretend to be models, and we would do runway shoots in my room with her dad's digital camera. But that was pretty much the extent of it.

"What's in it for you?"

"I get to prove that I know more about the Hot List than anyone else. Well, except for the Listmakers," I said, shrugging.

"I get it, I think," said Squid. "Maybe I'll do it."

"I'll take that as a yes. But you can't tell anyone I'm helping you to get onto the Hot List. Got it?"

"What about them?" He flicked his eyes over to Elio and Gabriel, who had been progressively creeping closer to us.

"NO!" I boomed, and they both ducked like I was going to take a swing at them.

"But they're my friends."

"This works much better if you can concentrate full-time and not get distracted. If the entire school knows what we are up to, then it'll be much harder, trust me."

"Aw, c'mon," said Squid. "Please? Double please?"

"Squid," Gabriel called from down the hall. "Elio's scrounging the dirt off your locker and making a beard with it."

Elio grinned at us. He had smeared the dirt all over his face in some sort of third-grade approximation of a beard.

"See," I said.

"You have a point," said Squid.

Chapter Thirteen

*S*ophie. *J'ai faim!"* says Squid, rubbing his hands together. *"Pour le kiss."*

I shut my eyes and scrunch up my face. "Never!"

"Calmez-vous," says Madame Kearns, narrowing her eyes at me and putting her fingers to her lips.

Hayden, who sits three rows in front of me, turns around and laughs. My stomach clenches. He is not laughing at me. He is laughing at Squid. He can't be associating kiss and Sophie and Squid because I clearly said, "Never" and said it in English so there was no confusion.

—Nightmare French conversation dreamed by
Sophie Fanuchi

In fifth period my French teacher, Madame Kearns, who was as prim-looking as a porcelain doll, was firing questions at us about masculine and feminine nouns. She wore an Eiffel Tower necklace and rocked on her little black flats that had ribbons at the toe, the colors of the French flag. "*Écoutez, le pain* or *la pain?*"

Pain means bread but it's spelled exactly like pain, which was what I was in when I thought of all the work that I had to do with Squid in order to get him Hot List–ready.

"*Le* or *la?*" repeated Madame, with her hands clasped in front—fig-leaf position.

I raised my hand, and, of course, Maddie, my brainiac former best friend, was raising her hand higher.

So I stretched a little bit, and Maddie stretched a lot higher. Madame Kearns nodded at Maddie. "*Oui?*" She smiled tightly.

"*Le pain*," said Maddie. "Masculine." Nia smiled at her approvingly as if she had just solved world peace and found the cure for cancer.

"Bravo," said Madame. She turned to face the rest of us. "*Écoutez*, I want you to work with a partner, whomever is sitting across from you, and ask him or her about what they would like to eat for dinner. *D'accord?*"

I turned across the aisle to face my partner. That would be Squid. I wasn't sure whether this was good or bad.

Bon or *mal?*

Mal or *bon?*

He got a huge grin on his face. With his arm extended backward, Squid was rolling his pencil across his blank piece of paper. It was easy to see where he got his nickname, since he apparently was so flexible he didn't have any bones in his body. *"Bonjour, la partner,"* he boomed.

"Bonjour, le Squid," I said back.

"Remember to say *le pain*. Not *la*," cautioned Madame Kearns. *"Répétez après moi: le pain."*

The whole class repeated in unison, *"Le pain."*

Then as we started working on our conversations, I noticed Nia and Maddie whispering together and glancing back at me.

I was finding it hard to concentrate on asking Squid what he wanted to eat given all of the Maddie/Nia giggles. As they loudly whispered, I could make out the words "shirt" and "so sad," but that was it. Mostly, it was—laugh, laugh, laugh, and then stares back at me. I crunched down on my teeth as Squid fished his French textbook out of his backpack.

One more whisper did it. I whipped around and snapped at Maddie and Nia. "Shut up."

"I'm not hearing *français*," corrected Madame Kearns.

"Fermez la bouche," I said, which meant *shut up*, only in French.

Madame Kearns locked her fingers together and rocked forward on her heels. "Sophie, I appreciate you're speaking French, but that's not what I had in mind. So, pardon your French. I want you to turn around and talk to your partner, Henry."

Madame Kearns happened to be the only teacher in the school who called Squid by his first name. I had even forgotten that his real name was Henry. Squid was so not a Henry.

Reluctantly I turned toward Squid, and he told me, in French, that he was hungry. "Sophie, *j'ai faim.*" Actually, it was more spitting than French because, as he exaggerated the *f* sound, spittle flew onto his bottom lip. He was also wiggling his body and patting his tummy. I think some sauce was coming off on his hand. The hand with the orange Magic Marker on it.

Then for a moment, he turned, and I saw *exactly* what Nia and Maddie must have been whispering about—Squid's T-shirt. It was bad enough that it was a Power Ranger one with some holes, but there was red sauce smeared all over the side shoulder and some on his back. Sometime between fourth and fifth period, he must have smacked into a pepperoni pizza. Reminder to self: introduce Squid to napkins.

Today I had on my brown hoodie. Underneath I had

on a baby doll T-shirt with straps that were definitely *not* two inches thick.

I had to give Squid my hoodie, so he could cover up his scary T-shirt.

No, I couldn't do that. Then I'd be wearing only spaghetti straps in the middle of class.

I turned away and kept on staring up at *The Little Prince* poster that Madame Kearns had behind her desk, which showed a weird little kid who lived by himself on a planet the size of a hot air balloon. Squid looked like an even weirder version of the little prince.

I had to do something about that.

Kids were staring at Squid, as the holes in his T-shirt appeared to have grown larger. And the sauce, saucier.

I had to save Squid from himself. From that shirt. From his crazy mullet hair, and teeth with food stuck in them. He needed to get off of his weird planet. I would introduce him to the concept of a haircut, of dental floss. It might be wise to ban stringy-type foods from his diet.

But I could at least start with the shirt.

"You so need my hoodie," I stated to Squid as he contorted one of his legs in a strange position around the chair leg.

Madame Kearns, stood in front of the class, surveying all with her small French ears, which had earrings that look like the Arc de Triumphe on them. "En *français*," she corrected, glancing over at me. "Speak en *français!*" Jiggling her little gold charms, she placed her hands back into the fig leaf position.

I struggled in French to tell Squid that he needed my hoodie, but I managed something French-sounding and then said, "Le hoodie."

Squid sat up, his eyes grew round and moist. "I *need* your hoodie?" He leaned forward, peering at my sweatshirt.

"*En français!*" reminded Madame Kearns, who was rocking on her heels even faster. English words definitely upset her.

Squid also mumbled something French-sounding and then said something like, "*Le cool.*"

I folded my arms across my hoodie, as if it were my life shield. Suddenly, I didn't want him to take it away. But it was the right thing to do.

Madame Kearns continued to survey the room, so I spoke in English under my breath, but with a French accent. "You. Must. Borrow. My. Le hoo-die."

"*Pourquoi?*" asked Squid, which was French for "why."

Everyone else was shedding their sweatshirts, sweaters, and hoodies, since it was practically ninety-nine degrees. The Administration at Travis—the administration being chiefly my father—believed in blasting the heat all winter long.

Nia had turned around again to get something out of her backpack, but I could tell she was just using it as an excuse to see what I was up to. She whispered something to Maddie. I wished I could put duct tape on Squid's mouth. But he'd probably just eat it.

"Trust me, Squid," I said, lowering my voice even more, but keeping up the French accent. "You just need my hoodie."

He stuck out his lip in a pathetic pout. I could see those bottom red braces, which clashed with his neon-green, glow-in-the-dark shoes. Nia and Maddie turned around at least twice and watched me. I didn't care what they thought, but I still didn't want them seeing me actually giving Squid an article of clothing.

I waited until Nia and Maddie were both facing ahead, looking at Madame Kearns's assignment that she was writing on the whiteboard.

"*Voila,*" I whispered, passing the hoodie under the desk, away from prying eyes.

Why was I doing this? Oh, right, the Hot List.

Squid snatched the hoodie and cupped it in both hands.

And that was when Maddie turned to peer at me. Her eyebrows curved into a question.

I flicked my eyes at Squid, who was frozen, still holding

my shirt. It was like he was meditating on it or something. Then he brought it up toward his nose and sniffed it before it putting it on. I cringed and my toes curled.

Okay, tonight, I was definitely going to have to sterilize my hoodie.

Chapter Fourteen

As I rushed down the hall, Maddie and Nia caught up to me.

"We weren't laughing at you in French," said Maddie.

I continued to speed-walk, keeping my eyes on the floor. "Okay, whatever."

"Nice top," said Nia.

"But you're going to get busted," said Maddie.

Nia nodded. It was true. Without my hoodie, I was only my wearing a tank top with spaghetti-thin straps. It was completely illegal at Travis. Straps had to be two and half inches thick, and you were allowed to show skin only two inches below your neckline. This shirt scooped big-time.

I tried to pull ahead of the Nia pack, but Maddie caught up to me. "We're just trying to help."

"Stop helping," I snapped.

"Seriously, Sophie," said Maddie. "Your dad does have a scary radar for anyone breaking the rules," she added, as Nia and then a frowny Ava pulled alongside of us.

"Maybe it's because of his radar ears," said Ava. "They stick out enough."

"Shut up," I said. It was one thing if *I* wanted to make cracks about my dad's ears, but not Ava. I also have this theory that whenever you say something bad about someone, you can guarantee they will show up.

I picked up the pace.

Maddie, Nia, and Ava picked up the pace.

I ducked my head down.

"Sorry about the radar-ears comment," said Ava.

"Whatever," I said.

I turned around.

My dad, Edward Fanuchi, a.k.a. the principal of Travis Middle School, rushed forward, racing toward me as if I had just stolen his basketball—only we're not at the court, we're at school. Travis Middle School. The school where he's the principal.

I was walking down the hallway—me, the principal's daughter—in a tank top with straps that were definitely less than two inches thick. I was so violating the dress code.

And that principal, my dad, was heading my way, looking as angry as I had ever seen him.

I was busted.

"Sophie," he said accusingly, "*What* are you wearing?" He stared at my spaghetti-thin straps. His face tightened and his irises contracted. This was trouble.

Everyone in the hallway had stopped to stare at me, as if I was wearing a bikini in a snow storm. A crowd of skater dudes, and a flock of sixth graders, carrying giant posterboards about killer viruses. I mean *everyone*.

Including Hayden Carus, who looked me up and down, taking in my too-thin-for-school spaghetti straps. I could feel my ears burning at the tips, and red-hot heat spreading across my cheeks and blooming up my neck.

"Sophie, you're going to have to change into something more appropriate right now," Dad said. "This is a warning. If this happens again, you'll get detention."

Maddie fingered one her of her many layers, a mint-green sweater with the ying-yang symbol. It looked almost like the one that Nia had on, except hers was in beige. "You can borrow my sweater."

"Um, well . . . it's okay." I so didn't want to be rescued by Maddie.

Dad eyes grew bigger. "It's not okay."

Maddie pulled off her sweater and her beads clacked together. "Here. Take it."

Dad smiled. "Thank you, Maddie." Dad looked at me expectantly. "Put it on, Sophie."

Reluctantly, I took the sweater. Did I have any other choice? I slipped it over my shoulders. Since I'm way broader and taller, it was on the tight side.

Ava clapped, which surprised me, since I thought she was so into being bored and annoyed unless she was on a horse.

"Perfect," Maddie said. "It fits you really well."

Suddenly, I shivered and my stomach muscles tensed up. But it wasn't perfect. This was Maddie's sweater, which matched Nia's sweater, and it smelled like mango lotion. It smelled exactly like them.

Chapter Fifteen

I flopped down on my bed.

I couldn't fail with Squid.

There was so much to do over the next month, Squid-wise, and not that much time to do it. In my mind I saw his mullet hair, which was scarily uncombed and the sauce on his superhero T-shirt.

Ugh.

There was no doubt about it, I was going to have to do a complete makeover on the boy. I sat by my desk and brainstormed a list to make Squid Hot List–ready.

Do List For Squid

1) Take Squid to the mall so he can get a look at what's trendy.
2) Buy regular, non-superhero shirts.

3) Buy normal jeans that don't show the colored bands around his sweat socks.

4) Buy un-florescent, non–glow-in-the-dark-type shoes.

5) Be seen with cool people, such as Hot Listers—to up reputation.

6) Spread the word that he's hanging with cool types.

7) Act less goofy.

8) Act less spazzy and hyper around girls (and guys, too).

9) Find non–yo-yo playing, non–muddy-footprint-measuring friends.

10) Get rid of mullet-type hairstyle.

There was a lot to be done. I decided that I would spread things out and start with the first four items on my list, which meant going to the mall and getting clothes and shoes.

Over the phone, I explained to Squid that he had some work to do, like acting less hyper around girls and hanging out with people who could help, not hurt, his reputation, and that he needed a style upgrade. I read Squid the list and waited for his reaction. Apparently, I overwhelmed him, as he wasn't responding. Had I freaked him out? "Squid?"

"You said you'd get me onto the List, but you didn't say I'd have to have plastic surgery."

"I didn't say anything about plastic surgery. We're talking some basics."

"Surgery's next on your mind. I can tell. I'm a mind reader. And maybe one of those medieval devices, where you'd stretch me to make me longer. Ouch. Okay, I think I'm quitting this Hot List thing."

"Squid. C'mon. I'll pay for everything you need at the mall," I said desperately. "I've got a ton of birthday money."

"Hmm, let me think about it." I could hear him tapping his head. "Think think think think. How much birthday money?"

"Two hundred dollars."

"Whoa," said Squid. "Okay. But I also want a new game for my DS."

"I don't think so. I'm not going to spend all of my money."

"Oh, all right."

Huzzah! I looked outside my window. The moon was so bright you could see the Rockies almost clearly. "Meet me at the mall. The south entrance right after school tomorrow. I need to be with you to make sure that you don't buy, like, light-up shoes or Barney pajama tops.

We've got to make you Hot List–ready right away. We don't have that much time. One month."

Squid made a sizzling sound. "That was me becoming hot."

"Ha-ha," I said and hung up as Dad popped his head into the room. "That wasn't Maddie was it?" he asked hopefully.

"Nah. It was Nicole and Heather." Of course it wasn't, but I wasn't about to tell my dad that I was speaking to Squid Rodriquez on the phone.

Dad sat down on the end of my bed. "I know it's been hard with stuff changing between you and Maddie. I'm glad you're finding new friends." He smiled, and picked at some loose threads on my comforter.

It was funny, but after all of this time eating with Heather and Nicole, I did, for the first time, think of them as friends. That part was true.

Dad smiled. "I just wanted to let you know that this weekend, I'm going to take Mynah out for dinner after a concert. I'll be gone awhile. But on Sunday, I thought you and I could do something together. Maybe hit the slopes?"

"Sounds good," I said, even though on Saturday night I sort of hated the idea of, maybe, being by myself and watching a movie. I also was a little freaked out when Dad called Mrs. Tate, Mynah. It made her sound like a person or, actually, more like a bird.

Dad grinned so lines formed parentheses on either side of his mouth. He'd been so happy recently it was hard not to feel a little bit okay about the dating thing. And Saturday during the day, I was going to be so busy shopping at the mall that, hopefully, I'd crash early.

Squid and I were walking through the mall. Scratch that. I was strolling through the mall and Squid was racing through it. I noticed a rack of scarves similar to the one that Maddie had bought me in Barcelona last summer. The one that I had thrown away. On impulse, I wanted to go and look at them, but I kept on moving because I was with Squid, and I wanted to get to Driscoll's department store. They had a boy's section and a big sign that said, 50% OFF SALE, which was a good thing since I didn't want to spend too much of my birthday money on Operation Make Squid Look Hot.

On our left we passed kitchen goods, such as blenders and electric woks and cooking pans with a giant photo of one of the Iron Chefs over them saying how much better your food would taste if you used his kitchen stuff.

Squid slowed down to stare at the display. "I've seen that dude on TV. He's awesome." Squid started to hum the theme song.

"Squid," I warned. "Someone could be listening."

"Oh, right. Sorry. Sorry."

As we strolled through the store together, I could hear the ladies behind the makeup counter whispering. One winked at me. What could they possibly think? That I was taking my brother shopping, and they're admiring my big-sister responsibility?

No, that wasn't it. I heard one of them. She mouthed something that sounded like, "Aren't they cute?"

Blech! She thought that Squid and I were a couple. I looked around. Did everyone think that just because two people were the same age, and one happened to be a boy, and one happened to be a girl, that they had to be a couple? What was wrong with those people?

I decided to move ahead of Squid.

Unfortunately, he caught up to me.

Squid was wearing a Daffy Duck shirt. "Are you still wearing your shirts from elementary school?" I asked.

He gazed down at the duck with admiration. "What? It's a classic cartoon. Everything I own is classic. I've got a Godzilla T-shirt collection and all of the movies on vintage VCR. I could probably sell them for at least $10 on eBay, but I want something to pass on to future generations. Future Squids." He placed his hand over his heart. "And Squidettes."

"A whole race of you. That's really creepy."

He put his hand up over his head. "Together, me and my ten thousand children will rule the world and Godzilla, too."

"Squid, you seriously need help." I shook my head. "Let's work on upgrading your shirts and jeans, okay? And then later we can look for some new shoes."

On some racks, after finding out his size, I pointed out some decent long-sleeved shirts without weird sayings, ancient monsters, or cartoon characters. "Try these," I said.

Squid stood next to me and pulled a shirt out. It said, SOMEONE STOLE MY IQ.

"No," I hissed.

Squid put it up against him. "But it's funny."

I shook my head. "No writing. Unless it's part of a recognizable brand or logo."

He pulled down a cowboy hat with little purple feathers around the band. "Howdy, pardner."

This was going to be one loooong day.

"How about I go over there?" I pointed to the pants that were hanging on racks against the wall. "I'll look for jeans. Things will go a lot faster that way. Just remember. Keep it simple. A black T-shirt, or navy." I pointed, once again, to the jeans area. "I'm going," I said. "You look too."

"Okay, chief. But I want my money first. You promised."

"Why should I give it you? Can't I just pay later?"

"Because I'm impulsive and have no patience," said Squid.

"Oh, here." I dug two ten-dollar bills and a five out of my wallet. "Remember. I'm jeans. You're shirts."

He saluted me and sort of took a flying leap down the aisle, almost knocking into an emo teenager in all black.

The jeans section wasn't too big. Most of the jeans had weird stitching with threads poking out. But then, as I spotted a decent pair, I saw someone who looked very familiar. It was Hayden Carus—Blue—with his sea-blue eyes and great smile.

The Hayden Carus, the one who I had spent about a hundred hours thinking about, and staring at his Facebook photo, planning our first date, and, okay, our future life together. *That* Hayden Carus, live and in person at Driscoll's department store.

His blue eyes crinkled up, and he smiled.

And I thought, *What do I say to him? I should be saying something to him.* But it had to be the right something.

I couldn't say just anything.

It had to be something memorable.

But not *too* memorable. Not geeky memorable.

I walked slowly past him, thinking in my head, what I could say? *What's up? Hey, crazy seeing you here.* No, no, wrong. *Looks like it's shopping day*. Wrong. *Gong*. No stars on that response.

Hayden stood there, his hands jammed into his pockets, looking really bored and cool.

What did he think of me? He was number one on the Hot List. I wasn't even on the List. The List that I created.

I was moving slowly past him. I needed to stop at exactly the right place. Not when we were side-by-side, but when I was past him a little, like he was an afterthought.

"Hey," I said bravely.

He kept on staring at a rack of skinny jeans.

He didn't hear me.

Maybe he didn't want to hear me.

"Hey," I said again a little louder, almost like I was Squid and unafraid of what anyone thought.

He still didn't hear me.

He had earbuds in his ear. He was listening to his iPod. Oh, I could work with that. Wonderful! I hustled down the aisle and wrapped around to the other side. I stopped, so that I was now facing him. I used body language and waved.

He waved back.

Yes!

He took out his earbuds.

My heart thudded so loudly I was afraid that he could

hear it. Suddenly, the memory of Maddie's voice popped into my head saying, *He must really like you.* You don't take out your earbuds for just anyone. She had been always trying to encourage me as we interpreted all of the little things Blue would do.

Like right now he was smiling. Maddie would interpret that as a good sign, and I did too.

I smiled back and realized I wanted to talk to him. But what could I talk about with Hayden Carus? Hayden required perfection. The perfect conversation.

"So are you out shopping?" I blurted.

"Kind of," he said. "Are you?"

"Yeah. I'm just looking for . . ." *For what, Sophie? What would you be looking for? Think.*

"Jeans?" asked Hayden, nodding at the pair I was holding.

"Uh, yeah."

"Cool." He nodded over at the register. "My mom is exchanging something."

"Cool," I said, trying to be supportive but at the same time as laid back as Hayden. Then I realized he just said cool, and I had just parroted him. I desperately tried to think of something else to say, some subject that wasn't completely lame, when he kind of half-winked/half-smiled, and my heart did jumping jacks.

I knew it wasn't my imagination. He was winking at me. "Hey!" he said.

I realized he wasn't *hey*ing me.

He had been *hey*ing somebody behind me.

"Look who's here," said Hayden.

I whirled around.

It was Squid, whose face was peering at me. Specifically, his head was wedged between boys size ten and twelve Spider-Man pajamas.

My head pounded like there was a drummer banging on the top of my scalp. *Please go away, Squid. Hayden Carus is here and has seen us together.*

The Hayden Carus.

He might think I actually liked Squid Rodriguez. *Leave, Squid,* I telepathically tried to communicate to him.

It wasn't working, so I mouthed *Go* to Squid and flicked my chin.

"Did you just tell me to go?" asked Squid in his unquiet voice.

"No, I was just, like, go-ing. Myself. Now."

"Too bad," said Hayden. "I'm going to be here forever." He gestured at his mom, who had a stack of clothes on a counter to return.

Did he just say, "too bad"? That meant he wanted to spend more time with me. Insert *Hallelujah* chorus.

"Well, I don't need to leave right away," I said. "I can hang."

"Cool," he said.

I tried to think of further coolness to say to Hayden. Mentally I went through all of the things I knew about him. He had great hair that, with a head toss, flipped off his forehead. He had dimples that appeared when he smiled. He played lacrosse.

"How's lacrosse going?" I asked, since I couldn't exactly ask about his hair or dimples.

"It's good," he said, looking down at his feet. "Except it's not lacrosse season. But I still play some in the indoor gym."

Was he bored? Was I boring him? "Lacrosse is cool, with those sticks. We don't have those in soccer."

"Yeah, you definitely need sticks." He laughed and then leaned his head forward.

"But they're so small." I pressed my thumb and pointer finger together. "Weensy."

"That's the point. If the net was big, it wouldn't be any fun."

"But you'd always catch the ball," I said. "That counts for something."

Hayden glanced around, and I worried that he was losing interest. But then he flicked his eyes back at me.

"My cousin was a midfielder," I said. "I used to go to

all of his games." Okay, I went to one game once, when I was seven.

"So you like lacrosse?"

"I love-love-love it," I said before I could stop myself. For some reason, I was acting like Squid—just saying any old thing that came to my mind.

Hayden raised his eyebrows, like he was surprised by my sudden declaration of lacrosse love.

"I love it too," he said.

Oh, we've both said the word "love." I could feel my smile spreading across my face like peanut butter. Not like peanut butter, though, because that was deadly for me, since I was allergic. An undeadly, all-the-way-happy non-peanut-butter smile spread across my face.

As Hayden continued talking to me, I noticed that he had a mole next to his right eye.

I could have stared at that mole all day. Like, if this were my last day on earth, this was how I would spend it—mole watching.

I had never seen Hayden talk so much.

He was going on about how he wanted to be back in midfield, for some reason, and some kind of attack strategy, which he had learned last year at camp. And he wasn't glancing around behind him at all like there might be something more interesting back there.

I was nodding in all the right places, thinking, he's talking a lot. Just to me. And he could talk to me whenever he wanted because I love just watching him breathe in and . . .

"So you could if you wanted," he was saying.

"Could what?"

"Come to a—"

"Hey, Sophie, what do you think of this one?"

NOOOOOOOOOOOOOOOOOO! It was Squid, holding up a giant fuzzy shirt. It was like a leopard print.

"Squid, what are you doing?"

"Whoops. I thought Hayden had left. Sorry, Soph."

Soph? He had never called me Soph before. *Now* he decided to name-shorten? Then Squid put his arm around me. Squid had never ever put his arm around me, and now he did it very casually, as if every day, every day of the week, he, Squid Rodriguez put his arm around me, Sophie. Excuse me, *Soph*.

This was a catastrophe! Epic. If I were Nia, I would make an announcement about it during a seventh-grade leadership meeting:

Announcement: Squid did not put his arm around me! Ever. I did not sanction this event.

If I were Brianna, I'd be the perfect flirt, like how she was with Bear. And I'd kick Squid, and then grab Hayden's arm and put it around me, and then I'd pinch him or something. And then I would tell everyone about it.

If I were Sophie, though, I'd do nothing. I'd stand there frozen as a mannequin, while Squid put his arm around me.

No! I shrunk back.

Squid was slapping his leg. "Sophie's *such* a good helper. She thinks everything I buy is tacky, corny, and heinous. So I thought I'd scare her with this one."

"You guys are shopping together?" asked Hayden.

"No," I said at the same time as Squid said, "Yes."

"I was, you know, looking at jeans, and Squid happened to be here, so he's been asking my opinions," I explained lamely to a baffled-looking Hayden.

"Sophie has a lot of opinions," said Squid. And then he folded his arms in front of him, like he was my parent or something, and tapped his foot. "And we didn't just happen to knock into each other. You made me come to the mall, Sophie. You even paid me to come." Could he really be this clueless? Didn't he want to get on the List? Grrrr.

"Ha-ha, like that would happen," I said. "Like I'd pay someone to come to a store. That's *so* weird, Squid."

He shrugged. "Yeah, it's weird and that's the truth." He pulls out a ten-dollar bill. "See!"

I folded my arms across my chest. "That proves nothing. It's money."

Squid waggled his finger. "Uh-uh-uh. It's not just *any* money." He sniffed the ten-dollar bill like a dog smelling a bone. "Yup. It smells like Sophie. A little bit of honey and lots of lemon, too. Kind of like a cup of tea."

Then Hayden flicked his eyes from me to Squid. Squid to me, like something was dawning on him. Something I didn't want to even think about.

Raising his eyebrows, he said, "Well, I'll let you two do your thing." He drawled out the word "thing" so it sounded like "thang."

My thing. I didn't have a thing. Or a *thang* with Squid Rodriguez. I could have a thing, but it would be with you, Hayden Carus.

Then Hayden walked away.

From me.

And our life together.

When I was sure that Hayden was out of earshot, when he appeared to be a dot over by the counter, I said, "Squid, your life is *so* over. What was the deal with the arm around my shoulder?"

"Huh?" He pushed out his bottom lip and his little round cheeks fell. "You said if I want to appear Hot List–worthy, I should act less spazzy and that it would up my rep to be seen with, you know, someone decent."

"I didn't mean me. And especially not around Hayden."

"Ewww, someone's got a crush on Mr. Number One on the Hot List."

"No."

"You should have told me that you like Hayden."

"That's not something I talk about."

"I do," said Squid. "When I have a crush, I tell the world. Like right now. Did you know that I've had a crush on Maddie since third grade?"

Whoa! I jerked my head back in surprise. "Are you serious?"

"Uh-huh," said Squid. "No problemo for me to speak my mind."

"Apparently. That was why you told Hayden I was paying you to go shopping."

He shrugged, all innocent. "What? I was just telling the truth."

"You don't tell the truth, Squid."

"Is that one of your rules to get me onto the Hot List?"

"It is when someone cool is around."

"Someone like Hayden Carus?" He raised his voice and clasped his hands together.

That was when I poked Squid so hard that he sort of

tripped backward. Actually, he fell on his butt, but I didn't care.

"You never ever tell the truth in front of cool people like Hayden Carus. Pick up my cues, Squid. And go very far away."

Squid threw up his hands. "All right! Okay, next time, I'll make sure not to let my uncoolness rub off on you."

"There isn't going to be a next time. He was going to ask to do something, like go to his game."

"Lacrosse season is in the spring."

"So? He was going to ask me to something else. Hayden Carus. Hayden, who could easily be on the cover of a magazine because he's so cute. Hayden, who has taken eighth-grade girls to dances. Hayden, who was actually talking to me for a very loooooong time."

"So, go find him and tell him you'll go to his game, or whatever."

"Right. That'd be so desperate. I. Am. Not. Desperate." I pulled my hands through my hair. "You're so going to pay for what you just did, Squid."

He handed me back the ten-dollar bill. "Will this do?"

I took the money, and then threw it back at him. "You are the biggest idiot. The lamest person I've *ever* met. I'm done."

Squid blinked and gazed at me vacantly.

"Do. You. Understand? Go find shoes or whatever on your own."

"Okay," said Squid. "Fine. You're done. Then I'm done too."

"Squid, no," I pleaded, realizing that I've messed up. Sometimes I'm such an idiot. "I didn't mean it."

He threw up his arms. "Apologize, then."

"Sorry," I mumbled.

"Gotta be more clear than that."

Oooooooooh! I lunged for him, but he pulled back, before I could grab his neck. "Just forget it about it!" I yelled and sprinted as fast as I could to do the nearest Squid-free zone.

Chapter Sixteen

When I got home, my first instinct was to call Maddie. Even after all this time, I found myself dialing her number. I could have probably dialed it in my sleep. How many Hayden stories had she heard? How many Hayden sightings had I told her about? She'd always say stuff that made me feel good and pumped me up. I needed that kind of boost again.

That's why I decided to call Heather and Nicole instead. Not only would I call them, but I'd also tell them about the bet with Nia. Why not? I mean, after everything that I had been through, what did I have to lose?

And you know what? It was the right move because they were giving me all kinds of support. Exactly what I needed, even if they weren't Maddie.

"I can't believe it," I said to Nicole and Heather on a three-way conversation on the phone. I paced in the kitchen, eating stale pretzels because Dad never closes the bag the right way. "What are the chances that Hayden would be out shopping when I was shopping?"

"Not a lot," Heather admitted. "I'm sure you can explain, right?"

"Text Hayden," commanded Nicole.

"Sure, if I had his cell phone number, which I don't."

Nicole tapped her chin thoughtfully. "Then write on his Facebook page."

"I'll sound like a lunatic. It's too late."

"Sophie, you're being a drama queen." Weird. That wasn't like me. My stomach bunched up and I felt jittery, like I'd had coffee before bedtime. Not that my dad let me drink coffee, except on special occasions. "Now everyone probably knows."

"Nobody knows anything. Hayden wouldn't say anything. He's much too cool. Plus, it's not like he exactly talks a lot anyway."

But still, I was convinced the world knew about the mall incident. The idea of this bet was to show Nia what I could do. I was now mud at Travis Middle School. This was not what I had in mind when I took on this little— excuse me—I mean *ginormous* Squid challenge.

Heather and Nicole tried to cheer me up, but even after eating almost an entire bag of red Twizzlers, I didn't feel any better. And then I really didn't feel better when

Dad came into the room and announced that he wanted to take me to dinner tomorrow night.

That, in and of itself, wasn't so bad. The going-out-to-dinner part. It was who he wanted to take me out to dinner with that was the problem—Nia and her mom. And he wanted to take them to my favorite restaurant, Bar-B-Q. It had an open kitchen, stone walls, and smelled like mesquite wood. They had these ribs and roasted chicken that was so moist you needed, like, ten napkins, and the portions were so big that we always end up taking home leftovers. The place was perfect, and I didn't want to spoil it with some bad memories. But Dad didn't give me a choice.

Dad and I got there ten minutes early so we could sit in his favorite booth, inside by the fireplace.

"You okay facing away from the kitchen?" Dad asked, sliding next to me. He knew that I liked to watch the chefs working, and I guess he wanted to sit across from Mynah, so he could gaze into her eyes.

"Sure." What was I going to do? Tell him the truth? That I didn't want to be there, that I didn't want him anywhere in the vicinity of Nia Tate, now or in the future.

The waiter refilled our glasses twice, and Dad ordered us both iced teas, as we waited for *them*, and Dad talked about the chances of the Rockies next season. I pretended to be interested in baseball stats when Nia and Mynah strolled into view. They were both wearing layers of shirts, vests, and scarves over skinny jeans with heels—only, Nia had her usual stack of beads and peace-sign earrings, and her Mom had on a simple gold chain.

Mynah took off her long wool scarf. "So sorry we're late. The traffic on the interstate was awful. Wasn't it, Nia? It was because of the sleet. Yuck." She pulled off her lambskin gloves.

"Yeah. It was kinda bad." Nia tossed her corkscrew curls. "But it didn't help that we left ten minutes late, either."

Wow. Mynah busted by her own daughter.

Dad swatted his hand in front of his face. "Ahh, no biggie. We've only been waiting here five minutes, anyway." He smiled and glanced at me. "And we got some good chatting time in." I noticed that Dad was wearing his nicest wool sweater, and had put on a musky-type cologne. Normally, he NEVER wore scents.

"Actually, we've been here fifteen minutes," I said. "If you don't count looking for parking along Main." Wow, this honesty thing could be fun.

Dad stood up, took Mynah's coat, and patted the banquette next to him. "Sit down. You and Nia look nice."

"Thanks," murmured Mynah.

Mynah glanced over at me. "You look nice, too, Sophie."

"You do," said Nia, which surprised me. She was obviously trying to kiss up.

"Thanks," I mumbled, although it wasn't true. My face was blotchy from post-traumatic Hot List/Squid stress.

We ordered calamari and fried onion rings as appetizers and made small talk, or, rather, Dad and Mynah actually talked, and Nia and I both pretended to love looking at the menu. When Dad saw a principal from another Boulder middle school across the room, he hopped over and brought Mynah with him.

"Okay," I said to Nia, who was dipping her bread into flavored olive oil. "Guess it's just you and me."

"Uh-huh." She popped the soaked piece of bread into her mouth. Then she ate an olive that sat on the table as a pre-appetizer. "Oh, yum. This is good." Her eyes glanced at her phone, which made me want to get her attention.

I couldn't help but stretch the truth a little. Okay, a lot. "So, I'm making really good progress with Squid."

"Really?" Nia scooped up another olive. "I'm like, um, surprised, since his, like, essence is all wacky and weird."

"Yeah, he's pretty wacky. But I'm working on it. Soon he won't be recognizable."

Nia shook her head. "That would be so sad, in a way."

"Sad?"

"I dunno. Then he wouldn't be Squid."

"Isn't that the point?" I was starting to feel angry.

"Definitely, which is why I think it'll actually be impossible for you to win. You've got to be true to your essence." Nia fingered her crystal necklace.

"Oh, c'mon. Is Maddie"—I made little quotes in the air—"'true to her essence' now that she's all flowy and hippie-chic?"

"Yeah. Why do you think we're friends?" Nia sat up really straight, as if she were trying to will herself to be as tall as me. It made me sit up straight too, so I'd be taller and intimidating. I was surprised she didn't say "best friends." "It's the law of attraction. Like attracts like."

"So, are you saying that you picked Squid because I'm just like him?"

"Or maybe you want to be like him." For the first time all night, she didn't look bored. "You know, I want to be a therapist someday, but, like, the holistic kind."

"Holistic?"

"You know, someone who helps people feel better by treating their mind, body, and spirit. My ultimate dream is to work in a little town higher up in the Rockies and to run groups under the stars, where people could find their authentic, real selves and touch their, you know, 'inner magic' and let the universe do its thing." Then she laughed at herself. "Goofy, right?"

"Kind of." Whoa. I didn't really have any idea of what she was talking about. Okay, maybe I did. But I was much too practical to buy any of it.

Nia dipped another piece of bread into the olive oil. "That could be good for you, Sophie. My mom did it, and she figured out who she really is. That's when she left my dad." As Nia chewed, I couldn't help but think she was talking about Maddie and me. That Maddie stopped being friends with me in order to find her real self. I clenched my toes as I thought about it. It made me *so* mad.

But Nia didn't seem to be aware of how upset I was getting. She kept going on about her parents. "They weren't meant to be. My mom wants the white picket fence, the house. The whole suburban thing."

Did that mean my dad was the suburban thing?

"My dad's a ski instructor up at Telluride," she continued. "And does ski patrol up there, too. In the summer, he's a white-water rafting guide."

"Sounds fun."

"Yeah," said Nia. "It's pretty cool, if there's any water left in the Colorado River."

It's weird. Part of me wanted to stay mad, and part of

me was fascinated learning more about Nia's life. Her dad, who spent his summer days on a rubber raft and winters on the slopes, sounded so different from my dad, who always stayed in one place. He was even born in Denver, so he didn't ever move too far. I decided to tell Nia thanks for sharing when her cell phone rang, and she picked it up.

"Hey, Maddy Mads. It's you!"

I slumped in my seat and shredded my napkin as I tried to figure out their conversation. It was hard. Nia kept on going. "Yeah. Bigger. Bigger. Much bigger." I had no idea what they were talking about and it was driving me crazy. And it was rude.

Suddenly, it all became so clear that I had to help Squid. There was no other choice. The boy was getting onto the Hot List and that was all there was to it.

"I know it," said Nia in a louder voice. "I'm so bored too."

That did it. I grabbed Nia's phone away. Of course, it was the exact minute that Dad and Mynah happening to be walking back to join us. "I can't believe you just did that," snapped Dad.

"But she"—I flicked my chin at Nia—"was being rude."

"It would be nice if you said something first," said Nia. Mynah sighed deeply. "I don't get it. We were just saying, a second ago, how nice it was to see y'all chatting together and bonding." Mynah/Mrs. Tate looked at me. "Sophie," she said. "Why don't you give me the phone, and I'll put it in here for safekeeping." She tapped her pocketbook and glanced at her daughter. "Nia, you know better than to have a conversation in the middle of a meal."

"I know. But it was an emergency." She smiled at her mother and then at my dad.

Yeah, right. The only emergency she had was rubbing her friendship with Maddie in my face. That was it.

After the dinner finally ended, and I was done with the torture of eating with Nia Tate, I decided I needed a little vitamin Nicole and Heather.

At first we were all texting, but then I decided to call because I wanted to tell them everything in detail. So I told Nicole and Heather about how my dad had been dating Mrs. Tate for a couple of months. After I told them about my dad's dating life, I wondered why I had held back from telling Maddie. I guess a part of me thought by speaking about it, I'd be admitting that it was really happening. Neither Nicole or Heather seemed too surprised about my dad and Nia's mom being a couple, since, as Heather put it, my dad's pretty cute for a middle-aged dude with big ears, and Mrs. Tate was the prettiest single teacher. Heather also thought them going out together was cute, and Nicole wondered if Mrs. Tate was going to get a raise.

Of course, I also told Heather and Nicole about Nia dissing me in the restaurant and the holistic therapy stuff.

"She wants to do therapy," said Nicole, "because, I can guarantee you, she's been in therapy for years, so she thinks she's an expert. Most therapists were messed-up when they were younger. So you have messed-up people helping other messed up people further spreading messed-up-ness." Nicole knew about that stuff since her dad was a psychiatrist.

"Do you really think so?" asked Heather. "About Nia seeing a therapist? She seems too happy and flowy, right?"

"Oh, she's a huge fake," said Nicole. "I bet when she gets home, she flings off her love beads, chows down on bloody sirloin steaks and screams for hours."

"Stop it. That's so mean," said Heather. "Don't you think that's mean?"

"No," I said. "I agree with Nicole. I think it's all an act. I saw her eating calamari and she admitted to me that she likes to win. That doesn't sound very peace-loving to me. She's competitive. I remembered when she first came to Travis, she glommed onto Ava because she could tell she was, like, the queen bee at the time. And when you start hanging around with the queen, her reputation rubs off, and then when you start acting like you belong . . . well, you do."

"I think you've just discovered the answer to the universe," said Nicole.

"Thank you. I try. But I've got to get someone cool to rub off on Squid."

"He's been hanging with you," said Heather. "That counts, right?"

"Not quite the same," I said, as I could feel the necessity to go to steps five and six of the get-Squid-hot plan. Not only did I need to get Squid to hang with the cool crowd but also he had to let everyone know about it. So I said good-bye to Nicole and Heather and texted Squid about the plan. Well, first I ate humble pie and apologized again.

Texts sent and received on Sophie Fanuchi's phone:

 After Dinner

 Fanuchi House

 Boulder, Colorado

 USA

 Thursday, October 5

 Between 8:01 p.m. and 8:06 p.m.

 Central Time

Sophiegrl 8:01 PM October 5

Sorry

Squidster 8:01 PM October 5

Say it agn

Sophiegrl 8:02 PM October 5

Sorry

Squidster 8:03 PM October 5

Louder

Sophiegrl 8:04 PM October 5

SORRY!

Squidster 8:04 PM October 5

☺

Sophiegrl 8:05 PM October 5

so we r on?

Squidster 8:05 PM October 5

Y

Sophiegrl 8:06 PM October 5

Good. Cuz we're going 4 step 5 and 6 on my

get you Hot List.

Chapter Seventeen

*D*uring gym, I sat in the bleachers next to Brianna Evans, who was still moping about how Bear had cut back on flirting with her in homeroom. I tried my best to listen to her complaints, but it was hard to focus. The place was hot, stuffy, and smelled like sweat socks. And anyway, I was focusing on step five of the get-Squid-hot plan. I desperately needed to find some Hot Lister to rub off on Squid, who earlier in the day was actually looking semidecent in one of the shirts that I had picked out for him at the mall. And he was wearing regular-looking un-neon, un-glow-in-the-dark basketball shoes. Guess he had kept on doing some shopping in the mall. But unfortunately, Squid was also busy discussing the new superhero that his friend Elio had just drawn on a piece of notebook paper. The boy definitely needed some new friends if he was going to hotify.

My P.E. teacher, Mr. Panigopolous, otherwise known

as Mr. Pan, was busy setting up orange cones for relay races. He waved a cone at me. "Hey, Sophie. We're doing three-legged relay races for the next week. Tell your dad it'd be a great photo op for the yearbook."

Mr. Pan went into the teacher-who-was-very-impressed-I-was-the-principal's-daughter category. Plus, I'm pretty much the best female athlete in the class, which didn't hurt either. Normally, all of his enthusiasm embarrassed me, even if I felt proud at the same time.

He would say stuff like, "Sophie, why don't you demonstrate a layup for the other girls?"

Or "I wish that the rest of you people would put as much energy into your run around the track as Sophie."

Or "See how Sophie is touching her toes during warm-ups? Fingers to toes, people!"

But today, a plan was sharply coming into focus. I was now going to use my status as gym teacher's pet to my advantage. "Mr. Pan, let me help you set up." I raced down the bleachers.

"Thanks, Sophie." He handed me a stack of cones. "Just space them about six feet apart by"—he squinted his eyes—"the free throw line." He grabbed a pile of bungee cord kind of rope. "I'll take care of these."

"Mr. Pan, I have a suggestion," I said, as quietly as I could. Not that I needed to be quiet. The rest of students were all gabbing in the bleachers, and some of the boys, including Hayden, were fooling around with a basketball by the hoop nearest the door. "I think Squid and Nia should be partners. It'd be great to see those two cooperate, since they've been having"—I lowered my voice even more—"issues."

That wasn't exactly a lie. It was more like Nia just thought Squid was beyond hope. But I figured, if Squid were seen tied up with the number-one girl from the Hot List, it could improve his status at school, especially if they won the race together. They'd be seen as a couple, at least for five minutes.

Mr. Pan scratched his love patch. "Hmm, I'm all for getting kids to work things out. I'll see what I can do."

"Thanks," I whispered and walked to the other side of the gym to do my job. As I put down the cones, I listened as Mr. Pan explained the rules. "There'll be eight teams with two pairs each. Each pair has to get to the other side of the gym and back, all while being tied together. Fun, huh? This is an exercise in teamwork and cooperation." Then Mr. Pan began to put us into the eight different groups for the relay race. It looked very promising because Nia, Squid, Ruby, and Trent were all in group four. Then when Mr. Pan said, "Ruby, you're with Trent, and Nia, you're with Squid," I almost shouted *wahoo!* at full amplification, as I strolled back to join the students, who were all still sitting in the bleachers.

It looked like it was time to hype Squid. And I knew just the person to help me—Brianna, the gossip and former flirt. I sat down next to her. "They're so going to win," I said, nodding at team number four. "It's got Ruby and Trent, Nia and *Squid*. And Squid's, like, so limber," I loudly whispered to Brianna.

Brianna nodded in agreement. "So unfair, that team's got everyone."

"I know it," said Alba, a shy girl with white-blond hair who sat in the row in front of us.

Oh, yeah! I wanted everyone to see Squid as an everyone, not as a weird one. Maybe I was becoming a List-making genius.

"Sophie, you're an eight, along with Maddie, Hayden, and Auggie," called out Mr. Pan through his megaphone thingie. Immediately, Nia gave Maddie an I-feel-sorry-for-you look, but I didn't feel that way at all because I was with Blue.

"C'mon, people, hustle up," called out Mr. Pan. "Get with your group."

I moved down the bleachers and stood next to Hayden. Normally, I would never ever stand next to Hayden, but I had no desire to be anywhere near Maddie Narita, traitor and ex-friend. And if I were standing next to Hayden, maybe we would get paired together.

Unfortunately, that thought made my face go red. I could feel my cheeks flaming. Oh, why did I have to think embarrassing things? Why did I have to have such pale-colored skin that strawberried all of the time? Maybe Hayden would just think I was hot, I told myself, as in hot warm, not hot sexy. Although it wouldn't be a bad thing for him to think I was hot-hot.

As if he could tell that all of my thoughts were about him, Hayden said to me. "Hey, are you ready to win?"

"Oh, yeah, definitely." Whoops. Should I have said "definitely"? That might have sounded too eager or something. Nia was definitely not eager to be literally hooked up with Squid. For a moment, I thought I saw a dot of sweat dripping down her forehead. But it might just have been the lights. Travis was famous for its bad fluorescent lighting.

As Nia dragged her way down the bleachers, Mr. Pan motioned for her to move faster, so she picked up the pace. "Atta girl, Nia," he said. "I know you can be your normal, enthusiastic self. But you need to take off those beads. You know the rules."

"Sorry." She put her peach speckled beads onto the bleacher and smiled enthusiastically for a mini moment.

"Can I switch and be with Maddie?" she asked in a fake sweet voice.

No, then she would be with Maddie *and* get to be with Hayden and Auggie. *No, say no, Mr. Pan,* I telepathically pleaded.

"How about next time?" offered Mr. Pan, who suddenly became my favorite teacher ever. "Today, Maddie and Sophie are going to be partners." Okay, scratch that. I hated Mr. Pan. He was my least favorite teacher and needed to take a very early retirement.

Nia gave Maddie an even bigger I-feel-sorry-for-you look.

But it was me she should have felt sorry for. Maddie wasn't exactly coordinated. And she was the last person I wanted to be tied up with, doing teamwork. I guess Mr. Pan was taking my suggestion a little too seriously, about pairing some kids up together who had issues. He knew Maddie and I weren't exactly speaking with each other.

I grudgingly stepped away from Hayden and grabbed one of the cords. "I can tie us together," I said to Maddie.

"Okay," she mumbled.

As I bound my leg with Maddie's, I glanced down at her shoes. Today she wore a new pair of black converse high-tops with peace-sign shoelaces. I thought about saying something to her, such as *I like your shoelaces*, but I just couldn't. Because it wasn't true. I hated her shoelaces. They matched Nia's.

Then Maddie said under her breath like a warning, "Blue."

Huh? I turned around and, sure enough, Hayden stood behind me. "Are you prepared to win?"

"Oh, yeah," I said. "You haven't seen Maddie and me do a three-legged race before. We're awesome."

"Watch it!" Hayden called over to Trent, who played with him on the lacrosse team. "You guys are going down."

"Don't think so," said Trent, who was now tied to Ruby.

Then I leaned away from Maddie as much as possible, considering that we were tied together. Maddie was also doing the same.

So far, today was not going as I had hoped. Like right now, Squid was doing a little I'm-with-Nia happy dance. Which I didn't quite get since just yesterday he had told me he was crushing on Maddie.

Boys were so fickle, really. He should be loyal to Maddie. No, that was crazy. Why would I care about that?

"Me and Nia, yeah, bay-bee," Squid sang out, as he shook his hips. "We're a three-legged legend." Then he did a front handspring. Of course, he wasn't tied up with Nia—at least not yet.

"Safety first, people!" called out Mr. Pan. "Remember, you have to think of yourself as one organism." If Maddie and I were an organism, what kind of organism would we be? Probably a scorpion. Definitely venomous. "Once the first pair gets to the finish line, the last pair goes," continued Mr. Pan. "Whoever comes in first wins. Okay, people? Everyone should be tied together by now. Remember, it's just a simple knot, no cutting off circulation. I wouldn't want anyone sewn together permanently." He laughed at his own lame joke.

"I'm going to be tied to Nia," called Squid, as if the entire world didn't already know that. I was going to have to teach him a few principles about playing it cool. I realized I had told him he had to broadcast that he was hanging with cool types, but he had to learn to do it subtly.

"Hiya, Soph!" Squid called out, a big goofy grin spreading on his face. "Sorry you didn't get to be tied up with Hayden."

I could feel my face flame up. And why exactly had I let Squid know that I liked Hayden? I couldn't turn my head because I didn't want to see Hayden and see his probable look of disgust. This day was quickly becoming a nightmare.

Mr. Pan shouted, "During the race, I'd suggest holding hands."

"Don't think so," Nia said. She stared at Squid's hands, which were covered with doodles of little aliens in Magic Marker.

And I was definitely not holding hands with Maddie. No way.

Suddenly, Mr. Pan was screaming, "On your marks, get set, go!"

In our group, Hayden and Auggie went first, and they were creaming everyone by a mile, even Trent and Ruby. It was as if they had morphed into some kind of three-legged rabbit. As they crossed the finish line, they had a lead of half a gym length. "You guys have it," said Hayden, who was out of breath. Hayden, *the* Hayden. If people could define words, then he would define hot.

"You better keep our lead," said Auggie.

"No problem," I said.

"Easy," added Maddie, and that was when I remembered that she liked Auggie aka Square. She must feel as nervous as me. Although there was nothing to get worried about, since we did have that HUGE lead.

I could hear Hayden and Auggie chanting our names together like this: "Sophie and Maddie! Sophie and Maddie!" as if we were still best friends.

I tried to sprint, but I stumbled, and we began pulling at each other, wanting to go opposite ways.

"Teamwork!" screamed Mr. Pan.

"Grab her hand!" Hayden screamed as Maddie began to fall.

"Grab her hand!" repeated Auggie.

By "grab her hand," I realized, they meant Maddie's hand.

Only because Hayden was screaming it and because I didn't want to also fall flat on my face, I grabbed Maddie's hand.

But it was too late because we tumbled onto the gym floor. Nia and Squid, who looked like flailing human octopuses, actually pulled ahead of us, along with everyone else. Nia was holding Squid's probably wet, clammy, and full-of-orange-Magic-Marker hand.

Maddie and I got up and continued pathetically hopping along. Hayden was actually still cheering for us, but it was pretty much a lost cause. Nia and Squid were too far ahead. Why couldn't I have been Hayden's partner? It would have been the perfect opportunity to get some actual skin contact with him.

Even Brianna and Elio, who were tied up together, were beating us. I think everyone was beating us. Maddie and I were hopeless together.

All at once the chatter in the gym went on pause. As Maddie and I finally made it to the finish line, everyone groaned. Except for Mr. Pan. "Sophie, I could see you hustle at the end there," he said, even though we both know it was not so true. But Mr. Pan *always* gave me the benefit of the doubt.

"Next time, you need to actually work together," said Hayden.

"You guys suck together," said Auggie, groaning.

"I could see promise there at the end," continued Mr. Pan.

"Thanks," I mumbled.

"We crushed them," gushed Squid. He raised his arms over his head in a champion pose. "We're number one."

"We did it," agreed Nia.

I dashed as quickly as I could back to the bleachers and joined Brianna. "Nice job out there," she said, laughing. "Not."

I rolled my eyes. "Yeah, it was *so* much fun." Then I realized something: Even though I had lost, Squid had actually won.

Chapter Eighteen

In the cafeteria before I went to sit down with with Heather and Nicole, I passed by Nia's table after I got my hot lunch, and I saw Squid point at Nia and wink. "You and me, bay-bee. We were one unstoppable three-legged ma-chine!"

"You're hurting our ears," said Amber, who was the quietest of the Nia table.

"Sorry, sorry!" shouted Squid.

The girls at Nia's table all laughed and held up their hands to their faces and went, "Shun."

And then I could hear Ava saying something like "He's a little too excited."

"I know, it's so sad," said Nia. Okay, maybe step five and six of my get-Squid-hot plan wasn't working. Shunning was not a good sign.

When I put my tray down at my table with Heather and Nicole, I told them about the gym incident with

Squid and the aftermath. Nicole opened her thermos of soup. "What are you going to do now?"

I shrugged. "I'm not sure. I think I've got to move on to numbers seven and eight on my plan."

"What's step seven?" asked Nicole.

"Make him less goofy. And number eight is to get him less hyper and more chill."

"But at least Squid looks kind of decent today, right?" said Heather.

"Yeah, maybe," I said, as I ate my chicken salad sandwich. "But he's still Squid."

Nicole nodded. "Exactly."

So, somehow, I got Squid to agree to meet me at the library after school for some lessons in acting regular. It was usually open for students who wanted to work on homework and stuff.

Squid unzipped his backpack and pulled out his notebook, which was scribbled over in unintelligible script from another planet. Balled-up papers, a half-eaten chicken sandwich, a yo-yo, and a wrinkled peach rolled out onto the table too.

"Squid, did anyone tell you that you're seriously gross?"

"Sorry." He smiled. "But funny, right?" He rubbed his hands together.

"Squid. Focus." I peered up at the clock on the brick wall of the library. I had to be home in forty-five minutes for dinner. Tonight was takeout Chinese food night.

Squid picked up the yo-yo and did some kind of elaborate trick. "Can you stop with your yo-yo?" I said.

"Sorry, sorry." He snapped the yo-yo into his hand and palmed it.

Humming, Squid stared at the wall, and then turned to me. "I've had enough of the library. Can I come over to your house? Please. I want to see what a principal's house looks like."

"Your eagerness is really creepy. Don't act like you're excited by stuff. Uneager is much better than eager." I thought of Hayden. If I acted all eager, I was sure he'd think I was such a dork.

"You've got to look bored like this. Don't make your eyes get so big and poppy-outy. Slouch and then look past people when you talk to them. Like there might be something more interesting behind them." I thought of me and Nia at the restaurant. "Make them want to make eye contact with you."

I demonstrated for Squid, staring past him, which was a pretty easy thing to do.

Squid practiced it, but he made his eyes too big.

"More squinty. Not so alert," I explained.

"Okay, okay." Then he did it for a moment. He stared past me, and through me, and was completely unfazed and nonchalant-acting.

"Perfect," I said.

"But that was sooooo boring to be that way."

"It's what you have to do," I explained patiently.

"But if I want to go to your house, why should I lie? Why should I pretend that I don't want to go? Are you asking me to lie? I don't like to lie. Because I think it'd be cool to see where the principal lives."

"I'm not asking you to become a liar," I said. "You just have to be sly. It's like with my little cousin Forest. If I tell him he should eat broccoli, then he leaves it; but then I say, okay, you can't eat broccoli, it's just for big boys, he'll grab the plate back and start gobbling it up. It's called reverse psychology. You need to use it a little."

"Okay, okay. I can do that. No problemo. Want to watch me? I can nail that."

"And when you do speak, do like, just little bits. No complete sentences. Don't say 'No problemo.' And remember the not-so-eager-part."

"Okay," he said, rolling his eyes. "Whatev."

"But Squid. This is important."

Squid grinned and started cracking up. "See, I did it."

"Yeah. That attitude was right-on. Like, you're a little bit tired of me."

Squid yawned. "Boring."

"Exactly, bored and slightly sarcastic. But huge amounts of sarcasm would take too much effort. Just mildly sarcastic."

Squid shrugged. "Uh-huh."

"That's it." I jumped out of my seat. "This is a breakthrough!"

Squid didn't smile. He shrugged.

"You're getting it, dude."

He shrugged again. "Cool." He slouched down into the chair.

"Squid, I'm liking it. This is good stuff. You just need to remember to apply it. In school and out of school."

He looked at me a little confused. "All right, chief," he said in a bored, low voice. "Whatever."

He was almost scaring me. Suddenly, he wasn't completely Squid anymore.

At home Dad showed me a bouquet of flowers wrapped in clear plastic cellophane paper. "It's crazy," he said. "But now that I have a girlfriend, I'm seeing flowers everywhere. And I just have to buy them."

I took a bite of the shrimp with lobster sauce that Dad

had picked up from The Golden Lotus. Girlfriend? Did my dad just use the *G* word? I guess they had been dating now for three months, so it made sense. A few weeks ago I remember that Mynah/Mrs. Tate didn't want anyone to know anything about their dating situation. I guess since, technically, Dad was her boss, she didn't want anyone to think she was getting special treatment. "Girlfriend" sounded so regular and out in the open. Suddenly the shrimp stuck to my sides and clawed at me.

Dad flicked his eyes at the flowers. "They're fun, right?"

No, they were carnations. Red ones that looked dyed and cheesy. If he wanted to impress, he should buy her violet tulips. I needed to tell him how bad these were, but I wasn't going to do it.

Girlfriend.

No, let him suffer flower humiliation.

Luckily, the opportunity presented itself immediately.

After we finished dinner, there was a knock at the door. It was Mynah/Mrs. Tate.

Dad didn't look surprised at all. After he hugged her, he explained, "Mynah had to drop off Nia for art class." Great. With Maddie. The art class where they first met and "bonded" over watercolors.

"I'd love to see some of her artwork," said Dad, carefully hanging up Mynah's coat on a hanger.

"Me too," said Mynah. "So far she hasn't brought back too much."

That's because all she does is talk and goof off with Maddie, I thought.

She walked through the living room into the kitchen. Opening up the fridge, Mynah took out the Brita pitcher. Behind the pitcher was our turkey for Thanksgiving. Mynah and Nia were going to see relatives in Denver for Thanksgiving, so we didn't have to do it with them. I had that to be thankful for.

I watched Mynah fill up her glass. "Want some water?" she asked.

I shook my head. The filter had been in there forever and was probably poisoning the water, but I didn't say anything as she took a sip. I guess that was evil.

"If you're hungry, there's a salad from Whole Foods," said Dad. "The kind with those pecans you like."

"Yum," Mynah said, as Dad got the salad out for her. "Y'all, I won't say no." Since when did he get anything from Whole Foods? He called the place "Whole Paycheck." Usually he shopped at King Soopers. This was definitely somehow Nia's hypnotic influence seeping into my family. The thing was, I had actually been telling my dad to buy stuff like organic milk for a while because it was healthier, but he kept on saying it was a rip-off. So, partly, it annoyed me that the Tates had this abnormal influence over people, like my dad and Maddie.

Dad sat down next to her as I stood there feeling, suddenly, like a ghost in my own house. I had *no* clue that Mynah was coming over. Didn't she have a daughter? Nia? Why was I thinking about her? I shouldn't worry about Nia. Was I crazy?

Maybe suffering would make Nia more human. Nah.

My stomach twisted.

I didn't realize that he was going to put the flowers to good use so soon. Dad nodded over at the buckets of shrimp and lobster sauce on the counter. "Want some?"

"Oh, I'm good," Mrs. Tate/Mynah said with way too much hidden meaning.

Later I called Nicole and Heather to entertain them with stories about coaching Squid and then I started sniff-crying, as I thought about Dad and Mynah. Mynah and Dad. The truth. That they were officially boyfriend and girlfriend.

Ugh.

"What's wrong, Sophie? Tell us," said Heather.

"You have to," said Nicole.

"Okay," I said, sniffing again. And then I told them all about my dad and Mynah Bird.

I told them everything so fast that I started to babble. "My dad got her carnations," I said. "Red ones. They looked brown on the tips and cheesy. And he called her his girlfriend. She thinks carnations are cute. I have a feeling she's going to stay overnight."

"Wow," said Nicole. "Think how you could go through her folders at night and let everyone know what's going to be on the pre-algebra test."

"Now, there's an advantage for you, right?" said Heather.

"Not that I'm going to do that." But it did make me feel better, and the three of us laughed on the phone about me being the pre-algebra spy for the entire seventh grade.

Chapter Nineteen

As I strolled into the caf, I checked out what Squid was wearing. We'd had a four-day weekend because of Thanksgiving, and I was afraid that over that time, he might have reverted back, style-wise. Good, he had on his long-sleeved skateboarding T-shirt. There were no superheroes or zombies in sight.

But then I saw something that made my skin prickle and feel hive-y.

In the middle of the cafeteria, Elio and Squid and Gabriel had stacked a giant pile of Legos. Legos were cool. I mean, when I was seven I had actually gone to Legoland outside of San Diego, but that's because I was seven. This was middle school, and they were making spaceships and making spaceship-type sounds and laughing goofily about it. And everyone was staring and whispering at them, especially the Nia/Maddie table.

Legos. Really, that was one step away from building blocks.

Elio had some kind of master Lego builder T-shirt, as if he had planned some sort of geeky Lego-themed day. *No.* Everything that I had worked so hard to build would crumble unless Squid distanced himself from Elio and Gabriel and their heaps of little plastic toys that snapped together. Step 9 (Find non–yo-yo playing, non–muddy-footprint-measuring friends) of the Squid plan had to be activated, like now.

After lunch I approached Squid, as he was heading to put away his tray. "You're going to have to give yourself a little break from your pals," I whispered.

Squid's eyebrows looked like a giant *V*. "What do you mean?"

"Like today, during lunch with the Legos. If you want to get onto the Hot List, you can't be hanging out with a bunch of guys who bring toys to school like that. You know about step eight of the plan."

"Do we have to do that?"

I nodded. "Uh-huh." As the bell rang, everyone began getting ready to leave the cafeteria. A group of guys lined up in front of the trash can and pitched their milk cartons into the trash like they were shooting hoops. One of the cartons bounced off my shoulder and a little bit of chocolate milk spilled out.

"Sorry," said the guy who did it. I thought his name was Sergio.

"Whatever." I grabbed a napkin off my tray and mopped up the spilled milk.

"You should have licked it off," said Squid, laughing too loudly.

"No. See what I'm talking about? You need to be around normal people who act normally." I flicked my eyes over at Elio and Gabriel who were scooping the Legos into Elio's backpack which had zombie stickers all over it. I lowered my voice. "They're influencing you to continue to act goofy and immature. It'd be better to eat by yourself or find some new kids to eat with. It'd just be for a few days. Squid, the List is coming out next Monday, one week. We're just talking five school days until December fifth."

"No," said Squid. "It'd hurt their feelings."

I leaned into him. "It's the only way. Look, it would only be if someone was around. Like, if you guys were alone in your house you could talk about superheroes, build Legos, lick chocolate milk, and walk up lockers all you ever wanted."

"You can't walk up lockers at home."

"You know what I'm talking about."

He glanced back at Elio and Gabriel, who were cracking up as they were flying one of their Lego-created spaceships into Gabriel's lunch bag. "I get you," said Squid.

"Just a few days," I begged. "Okay? Can you do that?"

"Maybe," said Squid. "I'll think about it."

"Do you or do you not want to get on the Hot List? Do you want to get whatever girl you want in this school?"

"I do."

"Then?"

"I'll do it," he said, but he wasn't smiling about it.

I guess Squid did some thinking, because the next day at school, he didn't eat with Elio and Gabriel. I wasn't sure where he went but he wasn't in the caf at all. Maybe the courtyard? Or the bathroom?

After school it had really warmed up and was a balmy fifty-two, which was pretty warm for Boulder, especially at the end of November. Since soccer season had just ended, I was staying after school and waiting for Dad so that we could go home together. I'd hang out in the library to do homework. But today I did my homework outside since it was so nice.

I noticed a couple of guys skateboarding over by the parking lot. I wandered over to get a better view because they both seemed pretty cute. One had longish dark curly hair that touched the collar of his shirt and the other had straight lighter brown hair with a mullet cut but looked cute.

It was Hayden riding his skateboard with . . .

I had to do a double take. Squid?

I mean it was Squid but it wasn't Squid.

Physically, it was still Squid. But when he glanced at me, the expression on his face was bored, just the way I had taught him. I had no idea that Squid could skateboard.

I was standing there for some time, and Squid kept on skating and high-fiving Hayden and all. Then I watched Elio and Gabriel also walk outside and stare at Squid. After gaping for a while, Elio called out tentatively, "Squid?"

Squid pushed his skateboard so it kind of flipped out from beneath his feet, twirled in the air and he caught it for a moment, and then it crashed onto the pavement. Okay, maybe he couldn't really skateboard. He had looked cool for about two seconds. But two very cool seconds, for sure.

Hayden stood next to him with his blue-blue eyes. For some reason, I noticed that he had a little ziggy scar along his chin. I thought it made him look tough in a good kind of way.

"Squid?" called out Gabriel. It came out as a question.

"Yeah," he said.

"I didn't know you skateboarded," said Gabriel.

"I dunno, kinda," he said.

"He doesn't suck," said Hayden.

"Whatever, I suck." Squid shrugged.

"One more time, dude?" asked Hayden, who glanced over his shoulder and smiled at me. At me. I felt a bunchy feeling in my stomach and didn't know what to do. Did he think that I was scoping on him or obsessed in a desperate way?

"I'm just on my way home," I said. "I had no idea you guys were out here," I said. Oh wow, that sounded paranoid and dorky.

I glanced over at Elio and Gabriel and knew they felt as surprised as I did. What were Squid and Hayden doing together skateboarding? How could Squid be skateboarding with Hayden. *The* Hayden Carus. My Hayden.

Oh, right. I had told him to find a Hot Lister to hang out with (step 6), and apparently that Hot Lister was none other than Hayden. I should have told him to pick someone else, because, well, when it came to Squid and Hayden, the embarrassment potential was high.

"You've got to show me how you did that last one," said Squid after Hayden did a Kickflip McTwist or something McDifficult. "'Cause I keep on blowing it."

Hayden pointed with his board. "You need more speed going into it."

I tried not to stare at Squid. What had changed? Mentally, I took inventory. Same small size, but decent-looking. But he was acting so uneager to see me and his friends that I thought I had entered into a different reality.

A Volvo pulled up and Hayden picked up his skateboard. "Anyone need a ride?" asked Hayden. He glanced around at all of us, including me.

"I'll go," said Squid. "But I'm calling shotgun."

Gabriel and Elio stared at Squid like he was an alien. "Aren't you staying after school for animation club?" asked Gabriel.

"Nah, I'm good," said Squid.

I pointed in the direction of my home. "I'm good too." I lived just a half-block away from the school. It would be so embarrassing to have Hayden's mother drive me one block. Then she would know, along with Hayden really and truly, that I was crushing on him big-time.

"See you," said Hayden. He nodded at everyone as he saluted good-bye.

"Later," said Squid.

Elio and Gabriel looked so depressed that they didn't even say good-bye, and in the pit of my stomach, I felt so wrong. I was making Squid abandon his friends just like Maddie had abandoned me.

And then I remembered. Squid was doing everything that I had asked him to do. I should be feeling pure pride, joy. Not panic. Inside I felt as if I were being split apart. I tried to knead the panic like it was dough that I could shape any way that I wanted to, only it wasn't working.

Chapter Twenty

Mrs. Casey, my English teacher, was asking questions about nouns. "Here's one everyone can answer," she said in her bizarrely slow manner. It was like she had gum in her mouth and didn't want to open it too much in case any of the flavor escaped. Actually she did have gum in her mouth. A little red stick of cinnamon the same color as her hair. You could smell the gum all the way in the back of the class where I sat.

The back of the class was the only place I felt comfortable because I didn't have to watch Maddie chatting with Nia. And Ava. And breathy-quiet McKenzie. And, well, anyone except for me.

Mrs. Casey chewed for a few moments and then paused. "Nouns can be person, places, or . . ." Things, of course. Mrs. Casey didn't care too much about prepping for class, which was cool because I could relax in the back and still do well.

Everyone was raising their hands. Except for Squid. He was kicking back in his chair, trying to be cool like I had taught him. He wasn't sitting with Elio and Gabriel.

I thought about the old Squid. The old Squid would have been silly and would be raising his hand as high as he could, which would probably mean standing on tiptoe or something or even on a chair.

He would have been shouting out the answer already: "Thing!" And saying when he grew up, he wanted to be one. A thing, that is.

But the new and improved Squid was yawning. And he was just about how I needed him to be to get onto the Hot List, except for one thing. The mullet haircut had to go. I should have taken care of that weeks ago.

"Um, Sophie, so?" Mrs. Casey called out, smiling at me sweetly like she needed a special favor such as going up to the office since I had a personal relationship with Mr. Fanuchi.

That happened to me just yesterday. Mrs. Casey had forgotten to fill out some kind of paperwork for her homeroom and asked me to take the sheet down to my dad and beg forgiveness for being a little late since we were—she put quotes in the air—"related."

"Do you want me to go the office?" I asked.

The class laughed. I tried to shrink down into my hoodie.

"I don't need you to go to the office. I had asked you

a question." Mrs. Casey tapped her foot slowly.

"Okay," I said hesitantly, expecting her to ask me if I was willing to read the weekly writing assignment aloud again, which I would not. That was something I always said no to. My voice shook whenever I read out loud in public. I stumbled over words and my cheeks bloomed strawberry red. And it had gotten even worse lately. Mrs. Casey peered forward and tapped her freckled nose. "Sophie. What's the answer?"

"The answer?"

"To the question."

Did I have my hand raised? How could she ask me? And how could I not know the question?

Maddie blew on her bangs and stared at me. She was probably upset that I got the privilege of answering.

I pulled my hoodie tighter around my face and slumped down into my chair.

"Sophie?" Mrs. Casey tapped her foot, which made a little clicking sound on the tile floor. "Have you been paying attention? Have you been listening?"

Mrs. Casey's head grew larger somehow right in front of me. I could hear the rushing of the blood in my veins, the beating of my heart so loudly that it drowned out any new thoughts trying to bubble out.

Pacing back and forth, Mrs. Casey looked like a hungry

cat. She furiously chomped on her gum. More cinnamon flavor blew into the classroom. Chatter erupted in the classroom. Maddie, who sat across from me, mouthed, *Adverbs*.

Why was she doing that? Was she trying to help me or mess with me?

Again she mouthed, *Adverbs*.

"Adverbs," I repeated softly.

"What did you say?" asked Mrs. Casey, whose mission in life was to get me to speak up.

"Adverbs," I repeated a little louder.

"Did you say 'adverbs'?"

I nodded.

Mrs. Casey spun in her chair and clapped, which was shocking since she never usually acted caffeinated. "Good," she said, smiling at me. "You have been paying attention, Sophie." She clucked her tongue. "For a second, I was worried that you had flown out that window and landed out there somewhere near Pluto."

My breathing was not so shallow anymore. Being the center of attention made my mind freeze like the rain sometimes does in April in the Rockies.

Mrs. Casey was now on to another question. Hooray!

Then Maddie smiled at me. "Thanks, Maddie," I said hoarsely.

After class was over, Maddie followed me into the hallway. She looked as if she wanted to speak to me but was waiting for something. Maybe for me to speak first? A bunch of seventh-grade girls who were all in band slowed down to stare at us. Their clarinet cases clunked into one another as they stopped short. Did we have to attract the entire marching band into our already crowded section of the hallway?

Yes.

Maddie pushed up her nose where her lavender glasses used to sit. And just as I was about to tell Maddie that she had forgotten she wasn't wearing glasses, Nia strutted over toward us. She waved her multicolor hairbanded wrist at Maddie. "Over here," she called out.

Maddie gave me a quick glance and then darted off to be with her best friend.

I pulled my hoodie farther over my eyes and imagined that it was a cloak of invisibility like in Harry Potter. The gaggle of band girls got bored and shoved off to watch other dramas. And I remained invisible girl.

Chapter Twenty-one

I needed to get Squid a haircut and complete the final phase of the get-Squid-on-the-Hot-List plan [10) Get rid of mullet-type hairstyle.]. It was Thursday already, and Monday, December 5, List Day, was fast approaching. After lunch I went up to Squid. "Whether you like it or not, after school you're getting a haircut."

He pulled on the tail of his mullet. "But I like my hair."

"Squid. Trust me on this."

"Sorry. The hair stays."

"I know a lot about hotness and even more about the Hot List."

"Whatever."

"Just believe me." I gritted my teeth. The new cool-talking Squid was irritating.

"No."

"If I tell you why I know so much about the Hot List, will you do it?"

"You mean like a Hot List secret?"

"Exactly."

"Then all right," said Squid.

Texts sent and received on Sophie Fanuchi's phone:

> **After School**
>
> **The Mall**
>
> **Boulder, Colorado**
>
> **USA**
>
> **Thursday, December 1**
>
> **Between 4:13 p.m. and 4:22 p.m.**
>
> **Central Time**

Sophiegrl *4:13 PM* December 1

I checked all 4 entrances don't see u

Squidster *4:13 PM* December 1

Im @ west

Sophiegrl *4:14 PM* December 1

Ill try agin

Squidster *4:14 PM* December 1

k

• • • •

Sophiegrl *4:21 PM* December 1

U r not here! Srsly

Squidster *4:22 PM* December 1

Look up!

Sophiegrl *4:22 PM* December 1

Get out of the tree!

On the way to the haircut place, Squid sprayed a tester bottle at the Cologne Hut, and the air smelled like lemons and watermelon.

I hated watermelon. More than peanut butter, even though that could kill me. If I had to be deathly allergic to anything, it'd be watermelon because it was so watery and weird crunchy with all of those annoying black seeds and white seeds to extra trip you up.

Out of the corner of my eye, I saw a guy leaning against the counter. He looked like Hayden. The same dark brown color hair. My insides flip-flopped. He turned around and the guy had zits all over his face and a weird handlebar mustache. Very gross and definitely not Hayden. Phew.

Squid was continuing to spray and pump the tester bottles on the counter, so that soon he smelled like every scent combined into one. "We can't waste time," I said since the haircut place always got crowded.

When we finally walked inside Hair Cutz, there were so many people inside the waiting area that some didn't have a place to sit.

"Are they giving something away?" I asked to a small man with a big mustache, leaning against a wall.

"Sorta," he says. "All haircuts are fifteen dollars. It's a good deal."

"Cool," said Squid, who pulled out a wad of ones. The old Squid would have said something like, *For that price, I can get two haircuts.*

I went up to the lady sitting behind a register counter. She had little stars on her long red, white, and blue–striped nails. "Do we take a number or something?"

"Just give me your name," she said as she chomped on her gum, which smelled like banana.

"Squid," I said.

Her eyebrows lifted in a question. "It's not my name. It's his name." I flicked my chin over at Squid, who was examining the hair products lined up on a shelf in the waiting area.

"Okay. Take a seat. If you can find one."

"Do you know how long a wait?" I asked.

"An hour at least."

"An hour. Wow." I shot back to Squid who had somehow managed to find a seat. He was flipping through a hairstyling magazine. "Look," he said, pointing to a photo. "I could get mine shaved like that."

"Are you kidding me? You need it cut normally—and to get rid of the mullet."

Squid pointed at a bald guy in a hairdresser's chair. "Do you think that guy really needs a haircut?"

"Maybe he's getting shaved in case the stubble is starting to grow back. The complete bald thing's a HOT look. But not the one you're going to get."

"If I ever go bald that's what I'm going to do, shave it all off."

"I don't think I'd like to see that. Look, I'm going to go into the mall and do a little shopping or something, so whatever you do, please, please wait for me. I don't want you getting a haircut without me. Call me when it's your turn, okay?"

"Fine," says Squid, saluting me. "So when are you going to tell me your Hot List secret?"

Suddenly, I chickened out. "Uh, later," I said. "I promise." Then I turned to the hairdresser closest to us. She had tattoos that peeked out along her neck and blue stripes in her black hair. "Do you know who's going to be cutting his hair?"

She shrugged as she snipped a girl with long blond curls. "Probably me or Becky." She nodded over at a hairdresser across the way with a shaggy-looking haircut.

I put my hands in a praying position. "Can you please, when you or whoever does his hair make it look, you know, regular? Like, get rid of the mullet, but no extreme spikes, no weird colors. He needs to look a little more average. But cute-way-above average. A trim. He needs help."

"You sound like his mother," she said as she spritzed her customer with a water bottle.

I stepped back and waved my hands in my face. "Oh, no, definitely not."

"A little young." The hairdresser smiled. "Don't worry. We'll make him look real nice."

"Thanks," I said, turning to Squid who was yawning.

"Just call me when it's your turn," I reminded him.

"You told me that already."

Ugh. He was so annoying.

And what was even more annoying was that the entire time I was shopping, I didn't hear from Squid. I checked my phone to make sure the ringer wasn't off. Nope. No calls, except a message from my network provider. It had been a little over an hour since I had seen Squid. I texted Nicole and Heather and complained about how slow the hair place was.

Then I decided to check in on Squid and surprise him. When I breezed back into Hair Cutz a ton of people clogged the sitting area. But they were all different people and there was no Squid.

I rushed up to the hairstylists with the blue stripey hair. "Where is he?"

"You mean your brother?" She nudged a woman next to her, sweeping up hair.

"He's not my brother," I said. "He's my friend." Was Squid my friend? I guess so. Yeah. "Kind of." I looked at my phone. "It's been over an hour."

"Well, your 'friend'—she used her fingers to make quotes—"is done. I fixed him up awesome."

"Before he got a haircut, he was supposed to call me." I stared at the woman's snake tattoo crawling up her neck. I peered at the blue stripes and her double nose rings. What exactly did "awesome" mean to her? Okay, I was fully frightened.

The hairdresser lady cupped her mouth and whispered confidentially to me. "I think he wanted it to be a surprise. He said he was going to the Apple Store."

He wanted it to be a surprise?

Oh, snap, I didn't like surprises, especially not when it came to Squid Rodriguez. I charged past a sunglasses hut, the cell phone hut, a restaurant where you pick out your own meat and veggies and they grill it for you, and, finally, the Apple Store, not that was hard to find, since there was a line snaking out of the place into the breezeway.

I stepped inside where hundreds of people were testing iMacs, iPods, iPads, and every iProduct imaginable. But most of the action was toward the back of the store where there were two long lines, one for support and another to make new purchases.

Where did Squid go?

And then I saw a guy, with bleached blond hair clipped shortish with a side part and long bangs that brushed into his eyes.

He was sitting on one of the long tables, fooling with the latest version of the iPad Touch. This guy was kind of cute, although a little short.

This guy was Squid.

No. Way. No, no way!

Couldn't be, but he was wearing Squid's clothes. So it had to be. Two girls flanked Squid's side. They seemed about our age, maybe a year older, and they were laughing and playing some game involving glowing creatures.

"Hey, Squid!" I called out.

He didn't turn to look at me.

"Squid!" I tried again.

He turned around, but stared right through me. The girls on either side scooted closer to him. What was he playing at? How could he ignore me? I made him. Who picked out his outfit? The cool one? Who took him to Hair Cutz? Me. That's who! That's when I screamed, "SQUID, C'MERE!"

Although I was standing about twenty feet away, I got my point across.

Squid gazed at me and twisted his mouth like maybe I was crazy. Maybe I WAS crazy.

This made me feel doubly irritated.

"Eww," said one of the girls. "Someone's in trouble."

"Someone is ticked," said the other girl.

Squid shrugged and stood up, but not before the two girls hip-bumped him. Then he made his way back over to where I was standing.

It was only when we were outside of the store, away from the groupies, that I got a really decent look at Squid. I had to do a double take. I mean it was Squid but it wasn't Squid. He had on the same T-shirt and jeans he had on earlier but with the haircut, it was like he was being possessed by the spirit of a cool boy. When he glanced at me, the expression on his face was bored. He has become the definition of "whatever."

I led Squid farther away from the perimeter of the

Apple Store and pointed to a bench next to a Hallmark store, and we both sat down.

"Squid," I said. "Why didn't you call me when you were getting your haircut?"

He shrugged. "I dunno. I thought it'd be fun to surprise you."

"Oh!" I clenched my fists so I didn't strike him, the new-improved-but-still-frustrating version of Squid.

Suddenly I realized that Squid looked great and that those girls were actually flirting with him. That I should be overjoyed, bursting with happiness with his new looks and personality. I appraised the haircut, the bleached blond streaks and the lack of a mullet hairstyle.

The two girls who were swarming him earlier in the Apple store did a "drive by" in that they yelled, "Bye." They strolled away giggling. These could possibly be the most annoying girls ever.

I waited for them to pass before speaking again. When they did, I said, "You're ready for school on Friday. And then on Monday, for the Hot List."

"Cool." With a bored expression, Squid stared at his fingers.

Chapter Twenty-two

On Friday, I was standing by my locker, when Nicole rushed up to me and cuffed me by the arm. "Look over there. Is that for real?" She was pointing to where Squid, the hotified version, stood by his locker.

Then Heather latched onto my shoulder. "Can't be, right?"

"Nope," said Nicole, shaking her head.

"Is," I said. "Told you." I had texted both of them in the mall right after Squid debuted with his new haircut.

We walked up to Squid, who was now shutting his locker and getting lots of stares from the kids passing by in the hall. There was no way that he wasn't getting onto the Hot List on Monday.

Nicole was the first one to speak to Squid. "Is that really you?"

"Uh-huh." He barely glanced up at them as he

shouldered his backpack. Down the hallway, I could see Elio and Gabriel, nudging each other and rolling their eyes.

"You look so different, right?" said Heather.

"Definitely," said Nicole. "It's hard to tell it's you," she said. "With the mullet gone."

"Whoa," said Heather. "Squid, you're kind of cute."

"Whatever," he said and turned away to strut down the hall.

I felt like a proud parent, watching her kid succeeding in kindergarten or something. But I was also watching him acting kind of mean to Heather, who was so sweet. And I was seeing Elio and Gabriel being ignored.

More girls approached, including a bunch of sixth graders who I didn't really know. And Maddie.

Squid flicked his hair back so it swept across his face.

Maddie patted Squid's hair and then pulled on it.

"Ouch!" shrieked Squid. "What are you doing?"

"Just checking to see if it's a wig," said Maddie, giggling.

"I want to check to see if it's a wig too!" said Heather.

"Me too," said Nicole.

"Us too," chorused some of the sixth-grade girls.

Soon a mob of girls were digging their hands into Squid's hair.

"OW! OW! OW!" hollered Squid, pulling away and putting his head between his knees, moaning.

Maddie held up a lock of Squid's hair and cast a glance at me like, *Congratulations, you did it.* How weird that Maddie thought I did a good job on my Squid makeover. I mean, wasn't she on Nia's team in terms of the bet?

"Not a wig," declared Maddie. "See!"

"I could've told you it wasn't a wig," said Squid, massaging his scalp.

At that moment, Hayden passed by twirling his lacrosse stick. And right behind him was Nia, Sierra, McKenzie, Ava, and Amber.

"Squid, is that you?" Hayden asked.

Squid grinned. "Uh-huh."

I turned to look at Nia's face. It was as white as Squid's blond highlights. Her mouth dropped open. She was blinking hard but, at the same time, trying to maintain her cool.

"Dude," called out Hayden. "You just had, like, a hundred chicks all over you."

"Definitely."

"I envy you, man," said Hayden. *Okay, rock my world! Hayden envied Squid Rodriguez. Whoa!*

Nia wrinkled her nose and scrunched her eyebrows.

Her nostrils flared and I could hear her huffing. Oh, she was mad.

Oh, my life was perfect!

Nia glanced at Maddie. "Coming?" she asked. For the past three months, Maddie always walked Nia to homeroom. I wasn't sure what happened to my brain, but I whispered to Maddie. "Stay." Just like that. Maybe it was because she seemed genuinely happy that Squid was succeeding, which meant I wasn't such a loser. Or maybe it was because I was in such a good mood.

"You go on," said Maddie to Nia. "I'm good." She turned to me as Nia sashayed away down the hall. "I guess she's a little mad."

"Guess so," I said.

"Even though Squid's only been hot for a day, I think he's getting on the List. Don't you?"

"You think?" I asked, my heart pounding.

"I do," said Maddie. "I really do." Then she leaned in to me and whispered. "I have a little confession to make. You know how on my original Hot List, there was a name crossed out?"

"Uh-huh."

"Well, it was Squid."

"Are you kidding me?"

"Nope."

"Oh, c'mon." I squinted my eyes at her. "Would you swear on truth candy?"

Maddie held up her hand. "I swear on all of the red M&M's in Colorado."

"Wow. Okay. Explain."

"Just right after you starting saying how weird he was, I crossed him off." She shrugged. "I felt a little embarrassed. You can be a little judgmental sometimes. But"—she grabbed my sleeve—"it's understandable. I mean he's a little bizarre. Or was. I mean he used to make me laugh and stuff."

"Used to?"

Maddie bit her bottom lip. "I don't know. He looks good. But he's different. Kind of like a lot of other guys."

"Sort of like you," I said. "Like how you changed when you got in with Nia and all them." Suddenly, Maddie shut her eyes, and she sighed.

"Did you have bring that up? Can you let that go?"

I shrugged. Could I? I wasn't sure.

In the hallways, during the break, Hayden gave me a long stare. I wasn't quite sure what it meant. But, maybe, just maybe, it was a good thing, or maybe not.

A moment later when Squid approached me, I was feeling so full of Hot List hopefulness that I decided to make his day and tell him about Maddie, which meant that I had to tell him about me—that I had started the Hot List with Maddie.

"We've got to talk," I said to Squid. I motioned for him to follow me under the stairwell.

"What's up?"

"Well, remember I promised I'd tell you a Hot List secret."

"Yeah?"

"Well, I'm going to tell you now." I took a deep breath. "Maddie and I started the Hot List. So, that's why, when I said that I knew a lot about the Hot List, I wasn't joking. I really do."

"Whoa." As if he was seeing a ghost, Squid looked both frightened and awed. "So you're the Listmaker. Like, you could put me on the List on Monday. I can't believe you didn't tell me on day one."

"Shhhh, keep it down. I'm not still doing the List. I have no actual idea who's doing it. But they're using my pen, which I threw away in the bathroom, that's for sure. Anyway, the point is the whole thing started when Maddie and I wrote up our own personal hot lists."

"And your number one was Hayden."

My face reddened. I could feel the heat in my cheeks.

"Go on," said Squid.

"Maddie put you down on her personal hot list."

"What number?"

"I dunno. Maybe like number seven or something. But the point is that you got on. *Before* your makeover or whatever."

"Awesome," said Squid. "Maddie, *the* Maddie, thought I was hot." It was funny, but Squid was sounding like me. How I talk about Blue/Hayden.

"Yeah, I guess so."

"Thanks for telling me, Sophie. You're going to be all right," he said, as he sloped away down the hall.

I'm going to be all right. What did that mean? I was already all right. I've never been more all right in my life. Sometimes, despite all of the changes, Squid could be so weird.

Chapter Twenty-three

Monday, December 5, List Day

Texts sent and received on Sophie Fanuchi's phone:

Before Homeroom

Travis Middle School

Boulder, Colorado

USA

Monday, December 5

Between 8:17 a.m. and 8:21 a.m.

Central Time

Sophiegrl *8:17 AM* December 5

Im so nervous

Cadieme *8:21 AM* December 5

No reason 2 be Squid iz hot ☺

All weekend I had thought about this day. Hot List Day. As I walked to my locker, I practically expected to see a giant banner strung across the hallway: HL DAY. But pretty much everything seemed normal except for the chatter, of course.

It was the usual stuff. "Do you think Nia's staying at number one?"

"What about Teddy?"

"I heard that Savannah might get on."

The usual stuff, except for one little thing. I heard Squid's name, and when I heard what was being said by a couple of sixth graders, my stomach squeezed up.

"I think the whole thing was, like, some kind of drama class experiment."

"I dunno, something. Because, look at Squid."

Okay, I didn't like the idea of the words "experiment" and "Squid" being uttered in the same sentence. I strolled over five rows to where Squid stood around with Elio and Gabriel. Whoa! What was going on? I thought that Squid had promised me he wouldn't hang out with them. They all had yo-yos in their hands and were performing weird and elaborate tricks.

Squid was snort-laughing, as Elio tried to get his yo-yo to walk up his locker. "Sorry, not working," said Squid.

Sure, Squid had a better haircut, but other than that, everything had reverted. Why? And then it hit me. I had stupidly told him about Maddie and how she had liked him when he was a complete dork. I was so dumb. Such an idiot!!! Squid was wearing his superhero sandwich shirt and neon, glow-in-the-dark green soccer shoes. The yo-yo was back and the snort-laughing. And he was with his dorkier side of dorky friends. "Squid, what are you doing?" I screamed.

"Walking up my locker. No problemo." He lifted up his soccer shoe. "See, it's good and muddy. Yeah, bay-bee!" Then he charged forward, slipped, and landed on his butt. Elio and Gabriel snort-laughed along with Squid.

"Squid, it's List Day!"

He turned around. "I know."

"I can't believe it. Go home and change. Elio. Gabriel. Can you leave him alone, just for a little bit more?"

"These are my dudes. Sorry." Squid waved at me. "Bye, Sophie Schmofie."

"Good-bye. Just like that, good-bye? After all that I've done for you!"

Of course, at that precise moment, Nia and her crew showed up. "Awww," I heard Nia whisper to Ava. "That's so sad."

Then Nia peered up at me. "I'm so sorry, Sophie." She glanced at Maddie, and Maddie glanced at me and shrugged like *I'm sorry too.*

I didn't want anyone's pity. I wanted Squid to get on the Hot List.

It was that simple.

Why couldn't my life be simple?

Homeroom crawled by as I waited for the Hot List to show up somewhere in school. During third period, I couldn't help glancing at Nia, who kept sneaking glances at Squid and shaking her head. The whole thing was making my stomach churn.

I overheard at least three bets happening between guys as we moved between classes to fourth period. Such as:

"I bet Micah Wong's going to move up. And Amber's going down."

"Dude, you're totally going to get schooled. He's going to stay in exactly the same spot. Same with Amber."

"Not. Bet you five dollars. Five dollars. How about your Xbox?"

Hands shook. "You're on."

And: "Did you see Squid?"

"Weird, huh?"

Understatement.

The Hot List had to be posted soon. First period had started, and everyone was waiting for news. I glanced down at my phone, which I had strategically hidden under my desk.

"I can't stand the suspense," I said to Nicole, who sat in front of me in pre-algebra.

She leaned back in her chair. "Oh, c'mon, Sophie. You know you love the drama."

"I don't think so," I said, as I tried to weigh the chances that Squid would actually make it onto the Hot List. I gave it about a fifty-fifty chance.

Mrs. Tate was giving us ten minutes of individual review time before the quiz, so some kids were still hauling their math books out of their backpacks while others flipped through their binders. Some girls glanced down at their hidden phones. I nervously snapped my binder open and shut.

Nia turned around and smiled at me. She fished out a blue-speckled mint from her backpack. "Here, have one. It's all natural and delish. I always love something to suck on when I'm nervous."

"But I'm not nervous," I lied, pressing my lips together to prevent Nia from force-feeding me some organic power mint.

Heather gave me a look like, *relax*. And Nicole shook her head. With my pointer finger, I made the crazy sign around her head.

Nia's face grew pink. Her cheeks ballooned and then she announced, "Sophie's got her phone out!"

My insides froze. I couldn't believe Nia would say anything, especially since she was stowing her cell in her lap too. I raised my hand. "Mrs. Tate, Nia has her phone out too."

Mrs. Tate drummed her manicured nails on her desk. "What am I going to do with y'all?" She flicked her eyes from me to Nia, and then from Nia to me. "Y'all are both hopeless." My heart whammed against my rib cage, and I silently pleaded, *Don't take away my cell on List Day.*

Nia must have been thinking the same thing because she clasped her hands into the begging poise. "Don't take it away. I'll do extra problem sets. Anything." She gave her best smile, the one that usually worked with teachers, and especially teachers that happened to be her mother. "Give me one more chance. Pleeeaaase?"

Mrs. Tate shook her head. "Sorry."

"Oh, please," I called out. "Give us a little break."

For a moment Mrs. Tate paused, and I saw a slight smile flicker. "I like to see y'all working together for a change. That's real nice. But the answer's still no." She approached my desk and set her lips into a line. "I have to take your phone. Hand it over."

Sighing, I gave Mrs. Tate my cell. She immediately imprisoned it in a drawer in her desk, then she took away Nia's phone and wrote our names up together on the whiteboard. "Y'all can pick them up after school."

Wonderful. I stared outside the window, where I could catch a glimpse of the mountains to cheer me up. After school I'd get my phone back. A lot of good that would do me.

Squid pointed to the whiteboard with his ink-doodled hand. "Ewww, Sophie and Nia both got warnings. They're like twins."

"Be quiet, Squid," snapped Mrs. Tate. "Or else you'll go up there too and then y'all will be triplets."

Nia shook her head at me like Squid was hopeless, and Maddie gave me another sympathetic look, which surprised me.

I dug out my binder, slammed it into onto my desk, and opened it to the pre-algebra section, marked by the blue index tab.

While Mrs. Tate watered her fica, the other kids were all whispering about the Hot List as they wrote down the assignment, which was in the right corner of the whiteboard. Mrs. Tate kicked some of the fallen leaves into a pile with the heel of her three-inch peep-toe heels. The kids around me were starting to pass the quizzes down the row. I stared longingly at the drawer where my cell was being held hostage.

Mrs. Tate clapped her freckled hands together. "Look

up at me, y'all. Remember this is a place of learning." A few kids snickered.

Not today, it wasn't about learning. Today was all about Squid and all about the List. And I wondered who was going to fall hard today. Me or Nia?

Chapter Twenty-four

*S*mall guy with big hair: Dude, Hayden's staying on as number one. And I heard Squid was going on.

Medium-size guy with a big backpack: Nahuh, dude. You better pay up on your bet. I heard Hayden's falling to two and no way is Squid going on the List.

—Overheard in hallway between first and second period.

As Brianna came down out of the bleachers in gym, she whispered in my ear. "This will perk you up. The List has been posted up by the lockers in the west wing."

I felt a little chill of anticipation. Travis, which is ginormous, is split into four wings: the east, the west, the south, and the north. The west is close to the cafeteria, which meant most likely there would be crowds the minute the bell rang.

My stomach lifted. I couldn't wait. I was praying hard that Squid was on the List. That would definitely mess with Nia. I wanted it to work out. It just had to.

As Mr. Pan spoke about the value of teamwork, I thought about how Nia getting off the List or being lowered, and Squid going on, would wipe the smirk right off her face.

I noticed Nia, who was sitting with Maddie, glancing down into her lap and smirking in a disturbing way. That was when Nia raised her hand. "Mr. Pan, I need the bathroom pass." Then she smiled extra big.

Oh. I. Couldn't. Believe it! She, Nia Tate, was using the bathroom as an excuse to be the first one to see the List.

Mr. Pan shook his hand. "Sorry, but Ruby has the pass." Mr. Pan limited bathroom usage to one at a time, which in the past seemed really harsh to me. For the first time ever though, I was enjoying his twisted bathroom pass policy.

"But it's been fifteen minutes," whined Nia.

Mr. Pan shook his baseball-capped head. "Sorry, kiddo. You'll just have to wait."

"But it's an emergency," she pleaded.

"When the going gets tough, the tough hold it in." Mr. Pan tossed up his baseball cap as he laughed at his lame joke.

Nia glowered at me as if Mr. Pan not giving her a bathroom pass was somehow my fault. As if his poor sense of humor was my fault too. That was when I raised my hand and told the biggest lie I've ever told during school hours. "Mr. Pan, I completely forgot to tell you. But I have to go down to the office." I looked at my watch. "In five minutes."

Mr. Pan's forehead wrinkled. "Your dad wants to speak with you?"

"Yes," I said, biting my bottom my bottom lip so I didn't laugh out of the sheer craziness of what I was doing.

"All righty, then. I can't doubt you"—he pointed at me with his megaphone—"of all people." He laughed nervously.

A-mazing! Mr. Pan was falling for it! I thought he might question me a little, but . . . nooo!

Oh, yeah, I was loving life right about now. But I knew better than that. I set my lips in a tight line and stared down at the bleachers. As I gathered up my backpack and stuff, some of the boys went "uh-oh," including Hayden.

But nobody made more noise than Squid, as he wailed like a police car in hot pursuit. Mr. Pan narrowed his eyes and vacantly gazed around the room, as if for a moment he was trying to remember how he ended up as a middle school gym teacher. "Um, Sophie," he called out, smiling like he needed a special favor. "Would you mind running up my homeroom attendance sheets? Darn forgot about 'em."

"No problem."

"Thank you so much." Nia furrowed her brow and shook her colored hair band wrist.

Mr. Pan was thanking me? And Nia was schooled? I loved it! I LOVED LIFE!

The perks of being the principal's kid. P.K. all the way!

Everyone was staring at me in an I-wouldn't-want-to-be-you way. But they didn't see my plan underway. Right now they were thinking that my dad wanting to speak to me meant I'd be the last person to see the List. They didn't get that I was the lucky one. It would be me, Sophie Fanuchi, who would be the first person to see the List!

Mr. Pan handed me an office pass and the attendance sheet. "Good luck, Miss Fanuchi," he said, bowing low. "And give your dad a big hello for me." And then he dove right back into his typical gym-type talk on cooperation and building trust.

I managed to keep my cool and breeze past everyone to the door. As the gym door clicked shut behind me, I faced the welcome silence of the empty hallway.

Chapter Twenty-five

I was strolling with my office pass when, suddenly, the silent, empty hallway wasn't so silent anymore. And it wasn't so empty as Nia pulled up right behind me. "Ruby came back!" she hooted, as she moved ahead. "So look who has the bathroom pass! Hee hee!"

Oh, snap.

Suddenly we were racing through the hallway.

I had the advantage in that I have superlong legs, but Nia had a head start. I moved ahead but I could feel Nia at my heels, which made me only run faster. That was when Mr. Roma, humming some heavy metal song, pulled up with his cleaning cart.

"Hold up there, girls!" He sternly looked from me to Nia. From Nia to me. "There is no running in my hallways. Both of you girls know better than that."

"Bathroom emergency," I said.

"Ditto," said Nia.

"Okay, but if you trip and fall, then you'll have a real emergency. Do you see the wet floor sign?" He pointed to a yellow plastic easel thingie.

"Got it, Mr. Roma," said Nia, giving her sweetest, peace-loving smile.

"See," I said, slowing down.

Nia and I gave each other a look, waited until Mr. Roma had turned the corner, and then resumed racing through the hall.

We passed rows and rows of pumpkin-colored lockers in the west wing. How were we going to find the right one? They all pretty much looked the same. We craned our necks this way and that, looking for an abandoned locker. At one point we heard footsteps but saw no one and both of us startled.

"The Listmaker?" I said out loud.

Nia shook her head so her spring curls bounced.

Then I spotted a locker that was slightly ajar and without a lock. It was next to a talent show poster that Maddie and Nia had painted together. A single tiny gold star sticker decorated the top of the open locker. Oh, yeah, this had to be it. Unfortunately, Nia saw the locker too at the same moment.

This time I had a head start, but Nia pushed me so I stumbled. We were sprinting neck and neck. If Mr. Pan had been around he would have been impressed and probably would have signed both of us up for the track team.

We slapped our hands against the locker at the same time, only Nia elbowed me and swung the door open, so I pushed myself forward. Together, in silence, we stared at the new List.

In that moment, I could hear my heart tick-tocking, Nia hoarse-breathing, the heater cycling on again and off again. On again and off again. It looked like Hayden had fallen to third place, which still didn't suck.

AUGGIE MARTIN
TEDDY STELLA
HAYDEN CARUS
BEAR ARVANITES
TYLER FINKEL
ANSON BLOVACK
MATT JAMES
NICK HYDE
ARI SILVERS
TYSON BLANDERS
GEORGE MCGOWAN
FRANK PARSONS
KIRK DAVIES
SEAN MCCARTHY

RANDALL TANNER
JONAH BARKER
BEAR ARVANITES
VINDAY PATEL
SERGIO RALETA
MICAH WONG

No Squid. Squid wasn't on. And I had lost. Lost! Lost!

"I'm so sorry," said Nia.

"Yeah, right."

"Keep on reading, though. You'll find the girls' list verrrrry interesting."

What did she mean interesting? I didn't like Nia's idea of interesting. My eyes slipped to the names on the girls' list.

NIA TATE
AVA ALLEN
SIERRA BLACKSTONE
MCKENZIE DARLINGTON
ADIA STILLER
AMBER SMITH
MEI WONG
ALYSON HERNANDEZ
SOPHIE FANUCHI

Whoa!!! Did I read that correctly? Somehow, I had made it up to number nine on the Hot List. How did that happen? I wasn't in Nia's glamour group. I didn't play girl drama games to get onto it.

"Congratulations," said Nia. "You're officially hot."

"But it's not like I was campaigning or something."

"Definitely not," said Nia, smirking, as I read the rest of the List.

MADDIE NARITA
SIERRA STEVENS
LESLIE GOTTFRIED
SARAH RUINSKY
JANE COCKRELL
LIESA SALEEM
CLARA PESSEREAU
SHERRY WARE
RUBY KUMAR
JENNY GOLD
LEAH PFEIFFER

I was trying to process that I got onto the List, when Nia broke out laughing again. "Guess you better prepare to wear that fuzzy boa, sparkly shoes, and tiara to school tomorrow," she said, "and look like an idiot in front of your crush. Hayden—I mean Blue, right?"

"Maddie told you that?"

"Don't be mad. It slipped. Should be an interesting lunch tomorrow."

I slammed the locker shut on a piece of my finger. "Ouch!"

But Nia didn't look back.

I barreled down the hallway and turned the corner. My finger throbbed, I had lost, and I was on the List.

I stood in terror as the bell to end second period rang, and, within minutes, hordes of students stampeded toward the lockers in the west wing.

Maddie headed the pack of mostly girls. They were moving at a fast clip down the hallway. As she approached, she called out, "Hey! I'm sorry you didn't win."

"Yeah, right," I said. "Apparently, news travels fast."

"Yeah," said Maddie, waving her cell phone. She probably got a text from Nia. I noticed she was wearing her lavender Barcelona scarf, which surprised me because I thought she was so done with lavender. And our twin scarves.

"I'm sorry about Squid not getting on," she said.

I turned to her. "Okay. Sure."

"Seriously. " She needled me with her elbow. I couldn't help it, but I started to cry. Not in an obvious way or anything. But I could feel my eyes getting all teary.

Suddenly, Maddie was hugging me. "You did a really good job, Soph. Seriously. With Squid." She was calling me Soph. Like old times. She whispered, "I know what you did. And it worked for a little. Squid, like, totally changed. But then he went back to himself," she said, shrugging. "Just with a better haircut."

"Yeah," I said. "Nia must be soooo happy about it."

"When I was heading here, I saw her skipping and singing down the hall. She did look pretty happy. I figured good news for her meant bad news for you."

"Yeah," I said. "That's about it."

After a few of the domino girls left the hallway where the List was posted, they passed by Maddie and me. One of them with short hair smiled at Maddie. I think her name was Crysta or maybe Chrisa. "I heard Nia's going to have a Hot List party?" Crysta/Chrisa said.

"Probably," Maddie said. "Maybe this weekend."

"Cool," said Crysta/Chrisa, who then left with her posse. And that made me remember who Maddie's best friend was and it wasn't me, even if for a second, we had a close moment. So I quietly scooted away down the hall.

I felt like everyone in the hallway was staring at me. A black cloud of awfulness had descended. And it had settled on me. My breath felt shallow.

Maybe I should go home and crawl under the rock of shame, I thought.

When the bell rang, I heard a cart clattering down the hall. It was the hall monitor Mrs. Heidegger with her walkie-talkie crackling.

The crowd immediately scattered. All except for me. I stood there dumbfounded. And dumb.

All of that work on Squid for nothing. Nothing! Maddie was still Nia's best friend. And it hit me. The reason I had done the whole thing, in a weird way, was to show Maddie that I knew more about something than Nia. Maybe I'd make up a new list for myself—a list of people with no best friend.

Chapter Twenty-six

Nicole and Heather called me twice, and texted five hundred times, to see how I was doing. The answer? Not great. For tomorrow, I had put a pink fuzzy boa into a bag, along with sparkly sandals, and a tiara that I had saved from a princess birthday when I was eight. It was too small and made my head look ginormous. On five separate little notes I had just written up the five things that I liked about Hayden. And each note, I had cut into the shape of a heart.

My embarrassing little heart-shaped notes:

I like how you don't carry around a backpack.

I like how you carry around your lacrosse stick because it means you're really dedicated and that's cool.

I like how your favorite candy is Jolly Ranchers because that's one of my faves too.

I like how you showed Squid how to skateboard, even
    if he's a goof.
I like how you asked if I was okay when I almost
    stapled myself to Mrs. McGibbon's desk.

I was pacing in the living room, with Rusty at my heels, when the door opened and Dad casually strolled through the door like it was just another day in the Fanuchi household.

"You're finally home," I said, sounding snappier than I intended.

"Sorry," said Dad. "Lots and lots of meetings." He looked at me. "So what's going on?"

"Do I have to go to school tomorrow?"

"Are you sick?" Dad put his hand on my forehead. "You don't feel warm."

"I'm feeling bad, trust me."

Dad put his hand on my shoulder. "Did something happen? Today at school?"

"No," I said. And that part was kind of true. "See, this thing that was supposed to happen didn't happen, and the thing that wasn't supposed to happen, did."

"Not sure I'm following you here. But you want to not go to school. I need details and facts."

"Those are the facts."

"Okay, when you're ready to talk, I'm here." He looked at me carefully. "Does it have anything to do with me dating Mynah?"

"Not really."

"That sounds vague-ish."

"It's not that. Mynah's all right."

We both sat there for a moment, not saying anything. All I could hear was the knocking of the heater and Rusty drinking his water downstairs. "But you're going to need to face up to whatever you're avoiding, okay, Sunflower?"

Sunflower was the name Dad called me when I was little. He always said I was as tall and beautiful as a flower that reached for the sun, and in that moment, I really wanted to roll back time and be that little girl again.

But I was a seventh grader, who had made a huge mess out of things and was going to have to face the cafeteria tomorrow in a tiara, sparkly shoes, and pink fuzzy boa. Hayden would think I was such a dork. And Maddie, of course. I already knew what Nia thought. And I thought I was a dork. By tomorrow even Squid, the king of dorks, would think I was such a dork. Wonderful.

The next morning Dad set a stack of pancakes in front of me. I gazed at them and my stomach twisted. "Sorry, Dad. Can you, like, save these? I'm just not hungry right now."

"Eat, Sophie," Dad said, putting on a silly Swedish

accent and pointing to the stack of pancakes. "I reheated them in the microwave from a genuine box."

Oh, wow. That explained how he was able to whip them up so fast. He nuked them even though he had put out whipped cream and chopped bananas and strawberries. I just wasn't in the eating mood. I forced myself to eat one silver dollar–size pancake, just to please him.

Then he pulled something out of his pocket. "I thought you might want this." It was the scarf that Maddie had given me when she went to Barcelona. The one that I had thrown away.

"But I thought—"

"I found it in the trash, along with some postcards, and I was thinking that, maybe, just maybe, you really wanted to keep it. And the postcards. I put them in my room, if you want them. As a memory."

I didn't know what to say so I said, "Thanks," and stuffed the scarf into my backpack, kind of for good luck. Because today, after what I had to do in the caf, I really needed some luck.

At school, Squid was pretty much doing the opposite of everything I had ever told him to do on my Hot List plan, except I did notice he had closed his mouth when he chewed his food when he whipped out a PowerBar.

Like in Mrs. Tate's class, he was singing the Spider-Man theme song, and the crazy thing was that Hayden, *the* Hayden Carus, started singing along with him, using his lacrosse stick as a conductor's baton.

Squid took out a Spider-Man pencil and swung it up and down like he was conducting an orchestra. Everyone was singing along. Mrs. Tate was laughing as she wrote up the whiteboard. Even Nia was smiling. But why not? She'd proven her point, and I was about to humiliate myself BIG-TIME during lunch.

Each time I glanced up at the clock, I was getting closer and closer to my little humiliation show in the caf. I put the fuzzy pink boa, the sparkly shoes, and the tiara in a bag in my locker. Today, time didn't go slow. It sped by.

Right before lunch I went to my locker to get my bag.

"Are you okay?" asked Heather.

"Not really," I admitted. "I'm going to have to work myself up to it." My stomach grumbled like I hadn't eaten in hours. Oh, right. For breakfast, I had only eaten one mini pancake. Somehow, I found myself standing in the line glancing over at Hayden's table, and Mrs. Daltry, the caf worker, was mumbling something at me. "Do you want a hamburger or do you want to continue staring at the boys?" she asked in her jokey way. "I know I'm not as good looking as those hunks, but . . ."

"What?" I stared at the meat loaf, and suddenly, I thought about becoming a vegetarian like Nia. "I'll take the bean taco," I said.

Why did I get that taco again? There was no way I was going to eat that. It had all of these little black flecks that were so random. I thought tacos were just plain tan. How come I never noticed that before? And I realized that there's a lot that I never noticed before. My stomach bunched up as I spotted Hayden, kicking a hacky sack under his table.

I went to sit for a moment with Nicole and Heather when I found myself face-to-face with Nia. "Ready?" she asked.

I fluffed my boa. "Uh-huh." I snuck another glance at Hayden, who was sitting next to Auggie and across from Trent.

"Awww, she's turning red," said Nia. "That's so sweet."

I could feel my face growing all hot, which meant it looked red and blotchy. And I could feel my hands shaking.

"Be quiet," I said as quietly as possible.

Then Maddie walked up next to me and lightly pressed on my shoulder. "Don't worry, you'll be fine." She smiled. "You look kind of cute." Was she trying to act nice? I hated how she kept being nice to me. It was so confusing.

She lowered her voice conspiratorially. "Blue will love the glitz."

"Blue?" asked Ava, who suddenly appeared next to Nia, along with Amber, Sierra, and McKenzie. I remembered that Ava had curly hair last year, but now she got it straightened and her hair flowed silkily on her shoulders.

"Blue is a guy who Sophie is crushing on," explained Nia.

"Yup," I said, thrusting out my chin. "Hayden Carus." Suddenly, I felt a little braver. Maybe because I was thinking about Squid in Mrs. Tate's class and how everyone was singing the Spider-Man song along with him. That he completely didn't care what anyone thought, and that was okay. Like right now, in the caf, Squid was doing yo-yo tricks with Elio and Gabriel. And even though they were knocking their chocolate milks over and stuff, you could tell they were having fun.

Nicole and Heather rushed up to me and my little entourage who were all eager to watch my Hayden humiliation.

"I can't believe you're really going to do it," said Nicole.

"Breathe, okay?" said Heather.

I felt the five little pieces of paper, each shaped in a heart. The five embarrassing things that I liked about Hayden. "I'm breathing," I said.

I expected Maddie to be smiling all smug. After all, I was about to about to humiliate myself in front of this entire school. Or at least in front of an entire cafeteria full of seventh graders. But instead, she whispered, "Good luck, Sophie" almost like she meant it.

Okay, that was it. "I'm going in." I put my boa on over my shirt, slipped on the tiara and the shoes. "If I'm going to do this, I'm really going to go for it," I said and marched, with my shoulders back, standing tall, right into the middle of the caf.

My stomach flopped and wiggled like the Jell-O on my tray.

That was when I started to self-talk. *I had been crushing on Hayden Carus for a while. If Squid could be Squid, I could have the guts to confess that I actually liked Hayden. Maddie didn't think I was an honest person in the feelings department anyway. And I didn't hate Maddie for this. I was thinking the same thing myself. I hadn't been real about my feelings. So, Hayden was a start.*

I stepped past the Quik Cart where they sold oranges and bags of chips. I kept my head up so the tiara wouldn't slip. As I was halfway across the cafeteria, Maddie raced up to me, yelling, "Stop! You don't have to do this."

"Yes, I do," I said. I pushed up the tiara. "I'm so doing this. I promised."

As Maddie stepped back, I waltzed up to Hayden's table, so I could face him front and center.

I took a big breath. I didn't gaze at his shoes, they might have been skater shoes or even those red Vans. I had no idea. I noticed his lacrosse stick leaning against his chair, and then I looked at his sea-blue eyes. I stood taller. I fluffed the boa. And I cleared my throat loudly.

There were a few "ooohs" coming from the table, but then mostly everyone shushed as I adjusted my tiara, which kept sliding down my forehead. "Do you like it?" I asked Hayden, as I tapped the plastic crown. Auggie and Trent stared at me with wide eyes.

"Um, yeah," said Hayden, looking baffled. "It's kinda nice."

"And my boa?"

"It's fluffy."

"And my sparkly shoes?" I hopped on one foot so he could see.

"They're definitely sparkly," said Hayden.

And then instead of talking, I sang. I actually sang out loud. I sang, "I wore them for you, Hayden!" Then I stopped singing and shouted, "Here!" I tossed the little red paper hearts, so they fluttered like butterflies over his head.

"Ewwww!" screamed Auggie and Trent at the same

time. They lunged to read the notes as Hayden swiped them off his head.

That's when I sprinted as fast as I could back to Nicole and Heather and Maddie and Nia and the rest of the girls who were all standing in one big clump.

"She did it!" exclaimed Maddie.

"I think I'm going to throw up now," I said, taking off my tiara and the sparkly shoes.

"You did great," said Nicole. "Honest."

"Definitely," said Heather. "I could never *ever* do that. You are so brave."

"Sophie! Sophie! Sophie!" chanted some boys in the back of the cafeteria. The chanting was started by Squid, of course. I glanced back over at Hayden, whose sea-blue eyes were now as round as pennies.

Hayden ducked as his friends threw the hearts at him, along with packets of ketchup and mustard.

I did it. And it was over.

Except not really because Maddie said to me, "I don't want you to panic or anything. Or act weird. But, Blue, incoming on your left."

"Got you," I said, nodding. Then I turned around and, sure enough, Hayden was strolling up to me. Oh, wow. Um. This time, I lost my ability to look right at him. Instead, I glanced down at the speckled linoleum, and then at his shoes. Hayden definitely had on those red Vans. I always liked those shoes.

Was he going to tell me that I totally embarrassed him, like, in front of the rest of the caf? *Probably*, I told myself. I tightened my stomach muscles and prepared for the worst.

"I like what you wrote," he said quietly, and that was all.

That he liked, actually *liked* what I wrote. I couldn't believe it. And then he smiled at me, a full smile, and his sea-blue eyes crinkled. Then he went off to catch up with Auggie and Trent.

Oh. This. Can't be happening. To Me. This is. *Too.* Good.

Maddie starting jumping up and down. And so did Nicole and Ava. Even Nia. Today, life was full of sparkles, fluffy boas, and BIG surprises.

"I'm kind of done with the Hot List," I said.

"Yeah," said Nia, smiling at me and playing with her clanking beads. "I know what you mean. You handled that really well," she admitted. "And I think maybe your crush likes you back."

"Thanks," I said. "I think maybe you're right." I didn't expect that from Nia. Not at all. Maybe, just maybe, she wasn't so evil after all.

Nia tossed her corkscrew curls. "You can take off your boa now."

Oh, right. I had forgotten about that. "You know what? I like my boa. I'm going to keep it on." As I retossed the boa across my shoulder, I could feel the feathers whooshing and tickling my neck, and, in that moment, I felt almost magical. Behind me, I heard what sounded like McKenzie, Amber, and Sierra mumbling something about getting their own boas at the mall.

And then another surprise came my way because Squid bounced right up to me. Actually, more than bounced. He did a front handspring in the middle of the caf and said, "I can't believe you did that. You stood up in front of everyone. You didn't care about looking like an idiot."

"Yeah. That kind of reminds me of someone."

He tapped his chin. "I wonder who that could be? Hmm." He was wearing his old crazy Power Rangers T-shirt, but somehow it looked cool and ironic on him now. "You know, you should really consider doing the talent show this year. You can actually sing."

"Maybe," I said. "I'll think about it." I paused a moment. "Sorry you didn't get on the Hot List."

"That's okay," he said. "But you did," he said. "That's awesome."

"I guess so. You never needed to get on the Hot List in the first place," I said suddenly.

"Maybe not. But I wanted to know what it felt like, and I decided I liked the old me better. When you told me about Maddie, I was all happy 'cause—digs chick me."

"I get it," I said, smiling.

"I missed my friends."

"I get that, too."

"And will you tell Maddie? That, I, you know, like her?"

"Since you're so shy?"

"Well, I helped you out. I figured you could return the favor."

"What do you mean?"

"That day, when I was with Hayden skateboarding, I sort of hinted to him, you know, that you liked him and stuff."

"What? You did *what*?"

"I figured I had messed things up for you earlier at the mall. So, I wanted to make it up to you." I was about to completely chew him out but then, at that exact moment, Hayden turned around and, like, winked at me, like he knew what we were talking about. Oh, this was good. And in a weird way, it was all because of the Hot List. The Hot List that Maddie and I started, and that someone else was continuing. Who it was, I didn't really know. Maybe it would always remain a mystery.

After lunch I caught up with Heather and Nicole and filled them in on the Squid and Hayden situation. To say they were ecstatic would be an understatement. We kept on high-fiving one another all the way to class. I thought about how eating with them had actually not been that bad. In fact, I had really learned a lot about them because I wasn't just relying on Maddie. For example, Nicole was really into anime films and had even got me seeing some. They're pretty cool. And she could memorize dialogue straight from any of the movies she had watched. And Heather did hip-hop dance and was really good at it.

"I can't wait for winter vacation," said Heather.

"I wish I was going someplace cool. Like Hawaii," said Nicole. "Instead it'll be the mall."

"Me too," said Heather. "But at least we'll be able to hang." She smiled at both Nicole and me when she said this.

Before the Hot List, I would have never thought of hanging with Heather and Nicole. But now I'm kind of looking forward to it, and I'm thinking maybe I could invite Maddie along. Who knows—maybe even Nia, and some of the rest of the girls. Maybe.

As the bell rang, out of the corner of my eye, I saw Brianna waving at me. She was about fifteen feet ahead, over by the water fountain. She was pointing at something.

"What's up with her?" I said, as she continued to silently move her mouth and make hand signals. "Seriously, what's up with her?" I said to Nicole and Heather.

Nicole shrugged. "No clue."

Then, suddenly, I got what was going on because I saw Bear throwing balled-up paper at her. He was flirting again.

"They're back to doing their thing," I said.

Nicole adjusted her backpack. "Apparently, your little display in the caf gave her the confidence to do her 'five things I like about Bear' in the hallway."

"Cute, huh?" said Heather.

During break between fifth and sixth, Maddie came over by my locker, and I noticed that we were both wearing our Barcelona scarves. I had put mine on over my boa after lunch, as a peace offering, I guess.

I pulled the scarf up around my neck. To me, it still smelled like what Maddie had said Barcelona smelled like—olives, fried potatoes, and those sausage thingies they plop on toasted bread. All of it.

Maddie waved her scarf at me. It was just like mine, except it was lavender, of course.

And I knew, at that moment, that she was still my friend.

Real life. Real you.

Don't miss
any of these
terrific
Aladdin Mix
books.

Ruby's Slippers

Home Sweet Drama

This Is Me From Now On

Devon Delaney Should
Totally Know Better

Front Page Face-Off

Nice and Mean

Do you love the color pink?
All things sparkly? Mani/pedis?

These books are for you!

From Aladdin
Published by Simon & Schuster

GET READY TO LAUGH OUT LOUD WITH THESE HILARIOUS BOOKS FROM ALADDIN!

FIVE GIRLS. ONE ACADEMY. AND SOME SERIOUS ATTITUDE.

CANTERWOOD CREST

by Jessica Burkhart

TAKE THE REINS
BOOK 1

CHASING BLUE
BOOK 2

BEHIND THE BIT
BOOK 3

TRIPLE FAULT
BOOK 4

BEST ENEMIES
BOOK 5

LITTLE WHITE LIES
BOOK 6

RIVAL REVENGE
BOOK 7

**HOME SWEET
DRAMA**
BOOK 8

CITY SECRETS
BOOK 9

Don't forget to check out the website for downloadables, quizzes, author vlogs, and more!

www.canterwoodcrest.com

FROM ALADDIN M!X   **PUBLISHED BY SIMON & SCHUSTER**